The Caves Can Hear You

A Somali Horror Story

By A.F.H

CONTENTS

PRESENT DAY

"Hurry up we'll miss our flight!" his mother yelled while the car was ready to take the family to the airport. It was the young boy's first time going to Hargeisa, and while the family were in the cab, the young boy looked outside of the window while they made their way to Heathrow Airport. The airport was filled up with families, also making their way over to the African continent. The family all sat in one row and went through the busy travels of passing through border security in Dubai; they then boarded the plane to the city of Hargeisa in the capital of Somaliland. When the family arrived in Hargeisa, a car had been waiting outside Egal airport. It was their cousin; He greeted the family and told them about the beauty of the city while he drove his Toyota Yaris through the city and the bumpy roads of Hargeisa. It was the young boy's mother and father's first time in the city before the breakout of the civil war, and this would also be his first time in a different country. He felt the fresh breeze of Hargeisa hit his face, and the sweat roll down his skin as he was now in the city his mother and father would tell him about back in England. They then finally arrived at his grandparents' house, "awoowe (grandpa) and ayeeyo's (grandmas) house" his mother would say they were going to, he knew a few words of Somali but not enough. The family left the cab and his mother and father hugged his grandparents tight. Tears and laughter erupted outside the family's home, they then made their way into the house and continued their conversation, they spoke about the memories before the war and the way so much had changed. Daytime then became nighttime and the young boy became bored and went into a room, he looked inside and saw an old man sitting there on a small wooden bed. "Kalay warya (come here)" said the old man. The young boy hesitated but made his way over to the old man, his room was clean and small, his window was also wide open. It smelled of uunsi (prepared incense) and he was wearing a white shirt and a macawiis (Somali male dress). The young boy sat down and asked the old man who he was, the old man then said he was his grandfather, the young boy then screamed "awoowe (grandad) and gave him a hug". "your mother and I will go out for quite a while, don't worry though your awoowo will look after you" said the young boy's father. As the young boy's father left, his grandfather looked into his eyes and took a book out of his drawer. "Sit quietly my grandson, I will read you a story you'll enjoy while your parents are gone, maybe you'll get in touch with your roots as I read this to you.

PART 1

HOOYO MACAAN

CHAPTER 1

COMING HOME

The day had begun in Hargeisa on the 23rd of March 1958, "wake up wake up, Aabo is home Abdirahman", said Majid as he kept pushing his older brother to wake up for what seemed an amazing day for the two boys. The family lived in a small 2-bedroom hut, comprising Abdirahman the eldest and Majid the youngest, they lived with their mother Sareedo as their father was taken by the British as a soldier abroad during WW2, he then became a seaman and travelled with the British ever since Abdirahman was born. Abdirahman had only ever seen his father once as a small toddler; However, now as a 5-year-old boy, he was excited to see what his father looked like. His mother always said his father was another version of Abdirahman, and this would excite him until this special day had come."Warya Abdirahman Nasir Zakariya soo kac warya (wake up) come and meet your father, he's waiting" shouted his mother. Abdirahman walked into the living room and saw a man, dressed in a blue shirt and grey trousers. His beard had grown until his chest and they could see him with a small army badge coloured in silver with the flag of the British protectorate of Somaliland. Abdirahman looked terrified as he did not recognise this man, "Hooyo, who is this" Abdirahman said, "this is your father" shouted his mother as she picked him up and put him on his father's lap. "Il waran (how are you)" said Abdirahman's father in a deep tone, "don't be scared Abdirahman, don't you know me?" Nasir yelled as he tickled Abdirahman, Abdirahman began to laugh and felt comfortable around this strange man he didn't recognise. He now felt at home and complete as his father told him stories of the countries he had sailed to on his expeditions with the British. They filled the day with laughter and joy, and it finally hit the time of Maghrib. "You know Abdirahman, don't go too far into the mountains of Hargeisa, there are xuux (monsters) there who will eat you if you are not careful," said Abdirahman's father. "He's only joking with you, that isn't true" laughed his mother. It terrified Abdirahman, as he heard the story of dheg dheer (fictional Somali monster) before and was even more scared when this was rolling off the tongue of his father. "Don't be scared, Abdirahman, when I go back on my voyage tomorrow morning, how will you look after the family? You will be the man when I'm gone," Abdirahman's father said as he laughed. Abdirahman's father reached into his front pocket and took out a shiny small box the size of his father's fist. The box looked ancient and had a shiny brown finish to it; However, it didn't have a lock to open it. It intrigued Abdirahman at this item. He had never seen such a beautiful object in his entire life. "What is that aabo?" Abdirahman said in amazement. Abdirahman's father told Abdirahman that this was a box given to him by a British officer from England. "Never forget to read your ayatul kursi (Islamic prayer) when you are leaving the house, read it for me my son?" said Abdirahman's father. Abdirahman read the powerful verse from the Quran. The night had finally been over, and the whole day the family had enjoyed each other's company Abdirahman's mother had finally gotten out of her seat on the warm floor, Abdirahman said goodbye to his father, as he would have to go back on his trip to the UK with the British in the early hours of the next day, he gave his father the tightest hug as he knew he wouldn't see him for a long period. As Abdirahman slept in his bed, the window was open, as the breeze touched his face he cried a little as he had just met and got to know his father that day. Fajr time (Morning prayer) had reached, and Nasir's name was called by one of the British officers. "Officer Nasir, let us leave We will be late for our ship in Berbera" shouted the British Officer. Officer Stevens was a tall, stocky pale man, sweating in the heat of Hargeisa's sun, he had a cigarette in his mouth as he loaded the car with Nasir's goods and ordered Nasir to hurry. "Give me a second I need to give something to my son," Nasir said. As Nasir ran to his son's room, he saw his son Abdirahman was asleep, he reached into his front pocket and bought out the box with a note reading "keep this box safe my son". He slowly placed the note underneath Abdirahman's bed next to the box, trying his best not to wake up his beloved son. He took one final look at Abdirahman and left with officer Stevens. He didn't know when the next time he would see his son was, but he had known he could survive without him. As the car went over bumpy rocks and potholes. Abdirahman's father looked over at the mountains outside of Hargeisa, as the two men made their way to Berbera, they stared into the tall mountains which could be seen on either side of their windows "what a beautiful site this is" whispered, Nasir. "Yes, a beautiful site I can see," smiled Officer Stevens.

CHAPTER 2

THE NEWS

The following day Abdirahman came back from school, he was ready for the dinner his mother had made for him that day. As he walked into the living room, he saw the clan leader and 3 women in the living room. He would only see the clan leader in their house when there was good news or bad news in the community. He suddenly saw his mother crying in the far corner of the living room. It confused him why his mother was crying, what could have happened? was it because his father had left again? He was asking so many questions about why his mother was crying, as she had never been the type to cry. She was the strongest person he knew, and he needed to find out why his mother was in such dismay. "What's wrong Hooyo," said Abdirahman, Majid looked at Abdirahman and shed a small tear. Abdirahman's mother took Abdirahman to one side and broke the news about the death of his father. She told her son how Abdirahman's father and officer Stevens had gone missing on their way to Berbera, however they found the truck stranded in the middle of the desert. Abdirahman could not believe what he was hearing; It was only yesterday he had last seen his father. He ran to his room and cried; However, he remembered what his father had told him and that was to be strong and to look after the family. Abdirahman slept with no dinner that night, and wondered how life would have been like if his father was still with him, after Abdirahman had prayed Isha (night prayer) he went to bed, that was the longest night Abdirahman had ever had as he struggled to sleep as he saw images of his father go through his head. Years had passed and Abdirahman was now 15 years of age, he began to grow in both his faith and responsibility, because of his family struggling to keep up with payments and money Abdirahman left school before he even finished. His mother had no choice but to support her son leaving school as once the British had left, they now united the country under the Somali Republic and finding any work after school was very difficult. As Abdirahman was strolling down the market of Hargeisa, he met his friend Abdala who was working as a loader with a truck driver. "How are you Abdirahman, have you found work yet?" said Abdala. Abdirahman responded and said it was difficult finding work and the only other option was to join the army. Abdala insisted that wasn't his only option, and he couldn't do that to his mother after what she had been through. He insisted that the truck driver Abdala was working with had a cousin which needed help on loading and offloading goods into Hargeisa. "You won't have to travel to Berbera, just offload the goods into Hargeisa" insisted Abdala. Abdirahman was excited and grateful for the offer and took it, as he went back to his house, he saw the look on his mother's face when he broke the news that he had found work.

You could see the struggle from the makeshift curtains and clothes they had made to protect themselves from outside in their small home. Abdirahman was now an offloader and went to work every day starting at Fajr and ending at Maghrib.

He wasn't paid much however this was more than enough than he ever thought he would get, he could finally provide for his family, while his younger brother stayed in school and his mother looked after the family home. Every day, as the trucks arrived in and out of Hargeisa, Abdirahman would daydream and remember his father, he would question himself. What if he was still alive? what if he made it from the desert? However, he stopped thinking about that and prayed his father was forgiven and granted Jannah instead.

CHAPTER 3

THE TRIP

The year was now 1972 and Abdirahman had just turned 17, there was a shortage of jobs in Hargeisa and Abdirahman was desperately looking for a truck driver after his previous truck driver had sold his vehicle and started up a small business. Abdirahman was left jobless and felt hopeless; normally Somalis would set off in pairs of two. One being the driver and the second person being the assistant offloader and loader. 2 weeks passed and still there were no truck drivers arriving in Hargeisa. Until a man named Sharmarke entered the city. Abdirahman asked him if he had any jobs; However, Sharmarke insisted he could cope on his own. Abdirahman begged and Sharmarke decided Abdirahman could tag along. Abdirahman asked Sharmarke where he was from. As Sharmarke was dressed in an odd fashion, and Sharmarke responded with "miyi" (countryside) Abdirahman asked what his tribe was, however, Sharmarke didn't respond. During that year, there were 12 cases of people going missing on their way to Berbera, and no one could identify the cause of this. Sharmarke who was a truck driver had the upper hand as he needed an assistant to load the goods when they reached Berbera. Abdirahman told the good news to his younger brother; However, his brother was sceptical of him going. Knowing someone's tribe was identification back then. However, Sharmarke didn't tell them his tribe or the area he came from. Abdirahman didn't listen as he would not want to miss this amazing opportunity. Sharmarke told him they would leave at exactly 9:00 pm and arrive before 1:00 am. It bemused Abdirahman as that was an odd time to leave. Normally, workers would leave at sunrise or after Fajr. However, Abdirahman was desperate and decided he needed the money, so they set off at exactly 9:00 pm that night. Before they left Sharmarke insisted Abdirahman also didn't eat or drink until they reached Berbera. Sharmarke, however, was tucking into baris (rice) and hilib (meat), the smell was horrendous. Abdirahman asked Sharmarke what animal it was and Sharmarke said it was camel meat. Sharmarke and Abdirahman then reached a petrol station, Sharmarke gave Abdirahman a new pair of clothes. As he insisted his old clothes were smelly and sweaty and Abdirahman accepted and changed. "Stay in the car Abdi, I will fill up the tank," said Sharmarke as he left the vehicle and proceeded to tell the petrol guy to fill up the truck. Abdirahman couldn't hear the conversation which was happening outside but continued to mind his business. When Sharmarke got back inside the car, Abdirahman could see the petrol guy from the rear-view mirror counting his money as they set off to Berbera, Abdirahman asked Sharmarke how he gained many amounts of clothes and shoes. Sharmarke said he came from a wealthy family in the countryside. While Sharmarke was eating his baris and hilib (rice and meat), he kept licking his lips and twitching. Abdirahman asked him what was wrong, Sharmarke kept saying "waan habsaamay" (I am late). Abdirahman also asked Sharmarke why he took so long to fill the car up with petrol. Sharmarke insisted Abdirahman went to sleep as he looked tired. Abdirahman thought this was a good idea and went onto sleep. Abdirahman awoke to sweat dripping down his face the car had stopped in the middle of the desert and Abdirahman was battled, as he looked through the window, he saw that the car had broken down in the middle of nowhere. Abdirahman looked to his left and Sharmarke was nowhere to be seen. Abdirahman left the car and saw Sharmarke changing the tire.

He asked Sharmarke what had happened to the car. Sharmarke said they drove over pieces of glass which ruined the tires. Now they were stranded in the middle of the desert. Abdirahman looked at the tires and saw that it was in good condition, Abdirahman was confused. Sharmarke looked At Abdirahman and smiled, as they stood there staring at each other, Sharmarke kept repeating the words "waan habsaamay" (I am late). Abdirahman Noticed three figures walking towards them, all dressed in black, they were also carrying a massive black bag while they approached the pair. Abdirahman was happy as he knew that they would help them with food and water and would hopefully help them make their way to Berbera.The three men finally arrived and greeted Sharmarke. Abdirahman was confused as to how Sharmarke knew these three men. One of the three men told Sharmarke "waad habstaamtay" (you're late). They also said they were very hungry and didn't eat for days. Abdirahman asked Sharmarke what was going on; however, he ignored him. Abdirahman started to scream louder at Sharmarke however he still ignored him. Sharmarke said, "This is the man I have brought to you today". Abdirahman realised what would happen to him.

The three men then told Abdirahman to come with them, or they would take him by force. Abdirahman agreed and prayed that nothing bad would happen to him. As they were walking Abdirahman noticed that the black bag they were carrying had blood dripping from it. He then realised where those missing people ended up on their way to Berbera. Abdirahman's life was flashing before his eyes as he continued to follow the three men to the destination, he accepted his fate but kept hearing his father's last words before he left to run through his head. Abdirahman then decided to fight back and threw punches at one of the men, however, the other two were quick to throw blows at Abdirahman. Abdirahman fell and gave up, he looked up, and saw that the three men stopped punching him, they shouted at each other and made an escape. Still confused, Abdirahman looked back and saw a beam of light. It was a truck, and the man at the petrol station jumped out from the truck "quickly get inside Abdi!" shouted the petrol guy as he helped the already beaten Abdirahman into the truck they then made their way back to Hargeisa. "I realised Sharmarke left part of his food in Hargeisa, and when I looked in the food, it was human meat!" said the petrol guy. On their way back to Hargeisa the petrol guy took an unusual turn. Abdirahman was confused, looking at the interior mirror he saw Sharmarke in the back seat.

CHAPTER 4

HOOYO MACAAN

Abdirahman felt lost, cheated and in a sense of confusion when he saw Sharmarke in the backseat. He thought he had made an escape from a nightmare; however, this was just the beginning. "Waan habsaamnay (were late)" Sharmarke kept repeating. "Hi there Abdirahman", said the petrol guy. "I would like to introduce myself; my name is Warsame". Abdirahman shouted at him and said, "I thought you're here to save me, brother". Warsame replied "no I orchestrated this for 2 months" as Warsame laughed to himself. Sharmarke was in the backseat screaming "Hooyo Macaan is waiting". "Amuus (shut your mouth) I'm in charge now, I don't want to hear another word from you," Warsame said. Abdirahman was left confused, "Who's Hooyo Macaan?" Abdirahman said. Warsame told him she was their leader, and she lived in the caves of the mountains outside of Hargeisa. Warsame also said that she hadn't eaten for days and that Abdirahman was her next meal. "We won't be long, so please sit back and relax brother, you were stupid enough to go with a stranger," Warsame said. "Those clothes Sharmarke had given you, were the clothes of past victims he also said". Abdirahman sat there, shocked and frozen. He was regretting everything he had done, regretting that he didn't listen to his younger brother and looking back and thinking if the money was even worth it. And now he would be on his way to the caves to meet with one of the most dangerous women he's ever heard of. "See I've been watching you for 2 months Abdirahman, I know your family and how you needed a job. I sent Sharmarke to you and I orchestrated this whole thing" Warsame said. Warsame also stated this was only business and he was not a cannibal. "I just work for these savages, and you are another product in the trade," Warsame said. As they got closer Sharmarke kept repeating the words, "Hooyo Macaan ba lagu geeyniya (you are being taken to Hooyo Macaan). Warsame had enough and knocked Sharmarke out. "He has been speaking for too long," Warsame said. Abdirahman was left in shock, Abdirahman asked what was wrong with Sharmarke. Warsame told him Sharmarke was taken as a child from Burco and was raised by Hooyo Macaan he also told him how Sharmarke had the mental age of a 10-yr. old. The group was now on the road for 2 hours and Abdirahman was still daydreaming about how his family must be feeling right now, but he kept believing he would get out of this nightmare. He kept praying and praying to Allah that it would work out. The group finally arrived at the destination, in the middle of nowhere they were surrounded by caves and bushes. They then reached a checkpoint, and a young female greeted them. "Waad habsaamtay". She said to Warsame, "next time you're late, Hooyo Macaan may have you as her next meal" she said. Warsame explained to the woman how they had an unfortunate accident on the way to the destination. However, the female gazed at Abdirahman, mesmerised she said, "but don't worry you have bought us something worthwhile". She told Warsame to exit the car and take Abdirahman to Hooyo Macaan, they walked up the staircase to the caves. The caves were covered with paintings and surrounded with around 8 different guards, both men and women wearing the old-styled Somali clothing and carrying spears. Abdirahman walked up the stairs scared for his life, Warsame kept pushing Abdirahman up the stairs and said they were close to entering Hooyo Macaan's cave. Finally, they had reached the top of the cave, and there they saw an overweight Somali female wearing an old Somali dress (dirac) and a red masar (red bandana). Her face had a numerous number of scars, and she had let her nails grow long. "my child, I have been waiting" she said. She shouted at Warsame and asked him what took them so long. Warsame told her how they had an accident and apologised as his life depended on it. "You're getting half your payment Warsame" she shouted. Warsame agreed as he didn't want to be another victim to Hooyo Macaan. Due to them taking so long Hooyo Macaan had already devoured one of her victims. "I am tired, take him to his cell warya" she said to Warsame. "I will see if I have enough room for him after tomorrow". Abdirahman was taken to his cell, a dark quiet cave far away from Hooyo Macaan. "You will sleep here tonight," Warsame said. As Abdirahman slept on the floor that night he felt a hand touch his leg. Shocked and frightened he saw a figure come towards him. "Don't be scared", said a young man. "My name is Ali, I've been here for 3 weeks, what is your name?" Ali said. Abdirahman told Ali his name and what had happened to him and where he was from. Abdirahman also noticed That Ali had a strange accent and asked him what city he was from. Ali stated he was from Mogadishu and that he had travelled to Hargeisa to visit his grandmother. "They ambushed me near buurta sheikh, I should've just stayed in the south" Ali kept repeating. Ali was a tall dark figure, with long dark hair and wide eyes. As they both sat there scared for their lives, Ali whispered: "don't worry aboowe (brother), we are escaping tonight!".

CHAPTER 5

THE ESCAPE

"I have been assessing the caves for weeks now, we are in the middle, Hooyo Macaan is at the top and the guards are below us," said Ali. Abdirahman was skeptical about Ali's plan however he looked to the view of the desert and knew it was his only shot at survival. "According to the sun it is subax (morning) at the moment, and we have no idea when Hooyo Macaan will get hungry. She normally feeds her leftovers to the guards or worse the dogs," Ali said. "Hooyo Macaan normally sleeps after her guards are done hunting after Maghrib (prayer) for wild animals, so we leave after Isha (night) Prayer,". So, the plan was set, Ali and Abdirahman decided to leave after the last prayer of the day. Suddenly they heard footsteps get closer to their cave and the sound of metal objects scratching against the floor. It was the female guard from the checkpoint. "I don't think I Introduced myself, my name is Idil and I'm Hooyo Macaan's guard and granddaughter. So, sleep until midday, before I tell her to be done with you now,". She left the cave with her long red dirac sheed rubbing against the floor her eyes were glancing back at the two prisoners. Scared and discombobulated, Abdirahman was counting down the seconds until they left this nightmare. "Don't worry Abdirahman were escaping 100%, I have a child and a family on the outside who are relying on me, I also need to see my grandmother as she is on her deathbed," Ali said. Abdirahman saw Ali not only as a prisoner now but also as a friend, a stranger comforting him was what he desperately needed. Ali kept saying "inshallah we will escape brother". Water was given to Ali and Abdirahman that day, as well as food. Abdirahman had not seen food for over 2 days on the way to the caves, so he ate and drank very quickly. Suddenly they heard footsteps coming down from the top of the cave, they saw a large female around 5ft11 inches tall, with a red Masar (bandana) and a dirac sheed (dress). "Don't eat so quickly, my child," Hooyo Macaan said. She then returned to her cave after staring at her two prisoners for a few minutes. The time was now Isha, and Ali and Abdirahman were waiting for their escape. They saw the guards disappear into the desert and hunt for the animals. Hooyo Macaan was deep in sleep as they could hear her snoring in the cave above. Ali woke Abdirahman up and told him it was time; they prayed and got ready for their escape. Abdirahman asked Ali how they would jump down from the second floor of the cave, "There is a rope next to Hooyo Macaan, she uses it to hang her workers if they misbehave, I will go up to her room and retrieve this from her while she is asleep". Said Ali. "You can't do this, you have a family, I'll do it," said Abdirahman. Ali refused and continued up the steps to Hooyo Macaan's room. There he saw the rope and Hooyo Macaan sleeping next to it. He tiptoed across the room until he reached the rope, which was on the left side of Hooyo Macaan's leg. He had been practising this for weeks and all this paid off. Ali successfully retrieved the rope from near her feet. He then made his way down to the second floor, avoiding any sound that would awake Hooyo Macaan and the remaining guards on the first floor. Once Ali returned to the second floor, he wrapped the rope around a piece of rock and told Abdirahman to climb down. "No", said Abdirahman "you go first". Ali responded with the following: "Please, brother, you need to go first. I will put my trust in Allah and whatever happens to me is Qadr. There is a camel down there we will ride west to Gebilay once I make my way down". So Abdirahman climbed down and saw Ali smile at him. Once Abdirahman reached the bottom the snoring stopped. "My food!!" screamed Hooyo Macaan as she ran down the steps in full force. Suddenly Abdirahman saw a red bandana behind

Ali, there she was screaming "cuunto!!" Before Ali could escape. She wrapped her big arms around him and dragged him away. She then saw Abdirahman was missing and looked down from the second floor and said, "I will be back for you Abdirahman!". Abdirahman shed a tear while he heard the screams of Ali while Hooyo Macaan devoured him. Abdirahman quickly rode the camel west hoping to reach Gebilay, crying his way there. Not only did he lose a friend, but he lost a brother. 12 hours had passed and Abdirahman was slowly losing his mind as he was dying for thirst, he collapsed from the camel in the middle of the desert. As Abdirahman lay there helpless, he saw a woman come closer to him from the distance; She was riding a camel, and he realised it was Idil holding her spear. Abdirahman gave up and accepted his fate. "You thought you could escape from us, didn't you?" Idil said as she picked him up and loaded Abdirahman onto her camel. A man who was riding a black horse then appeared from the distance. "What are you doing with this man," he said when he arrived. "He is my brother," she said. He knew she was lying and told her to put him down and come with him to Gebilay for questioning as the man could see the state Abdirahman was in. Gebilay was now only 1 mile away and could be seen in the distance. She would be questioned for why she was carrying an innocent boy. Idil realised she had lost, so she brought out her spear and threw it at the man. He dodged the spear and "bang!". Idil was shot dead on the spot. The man told Abdirahman he was a local police officer from Gebilay, and he would be taken to Gebilay for treatment and then taken back to Hargeisa to his family. Once Abdirahman was treated he was taken back to his home city of Hargeisa and reunited with his family, Abdirahman's mother cried and thanked Allah that her son was finally home after he had been missing for so long. An end of a nightmare had finally been over for Abdirahman, he was finally back in his room in Hargeisa around his friends and family that he thought he would never see again. Not only was he in pain from the ordeal, however, flashbacks of his friend Ali also took over his head. As he wept in his bed, the guests had left the house, his brother Majid walked in and comforted him. "The neighbours said you would never return, but I believed in you Abdirahman, I knew you would come back", said Majid. "That's enough now Majid, let Abdirahman rest he has been through a lot," said his mother, she gave him a kiss and proceeded to leave the room. Abdirahman laid there that night, frozen in time and remembering the nightmare he had witnessed in those caves. He did not tell his family members what had occurred in those caves; however, he was finally home and the nightmare had ended.

CHAPTER 6

THE MARRIAGE

The year was now 1975, Abdirahman was back up on his feet; However, the memories of what had taken place years before still surrounded his mind. He was strong, however, and had done well for himself. He had started trading clothes and jewellery in downtown Hargeisa when the torment was over, and over the years his business had flourished. He was also able to move his family out of the small home that they had struggled in for so many years. One day when Abdirahman was preparing to open his shop for the day, his eyes locked onto a beautiful young woman who was also preparing to open her stand across the busy road from him. As the day went on Abdirahman's eyes couldn't stay in one place, as it kept glancing over at this mysterious woman he couldn't stop staring at since he opened his shop. Medium in height, she was wearing a loose shalmad (headscarf) and a long dirac shiid (Somali dress) which touched the sandy floors of Hargeisa's busy market. Her stand did not have much, a few pieces of jewellery and books were piled on her small table. When the day was over, Abdirahman was determined to go across the road and introduce himself to the young woman. As Abdirahman finished closing his shop, he had realised

48

she left and closed before he did. As Abdirahman walked, he kept thinking about that beautiful woman he had seen today and kept regretting that he didn't approach her. The next day Abdirahman set up shop again and the same woman he had seen yesterday was there before him. As he continued to work and sell his items, the sand and wind of Hargeisa muzzled Abdirahman's view of the road and customers, once this was over, he could see the woman of his dreams right in front of him. "Why do you keep staring at me?" said the young woman, "II dd.." stuttered Abdi, before he could finish his sentence the woman said, "I'm only joking, I'm here to ask you to stop stealing my customers, they seem to be coming to you all the time". Abdi laughed "What is your name, and why don't I normally see you here?" he said as he stared awkwardly at her face and to the floor, while the sun was setting on Hargeisa, he was mesmerised as the sun set beneath her head. "My name is Sagal. I moved here from Borama with my uncle and brother. I heard there's a lot of opportunities here in Hargeisa" she replied. She also stated how her father and mother had passed away when she was younger and was raised by her uncle. "Ever since my parents passed my uncle has brought me up," Sagal said. "My name is Abdir.." Abdirahman was not made to finish his sentence a second time as Sagal interrupted him again. "I know who you are, and I've heard the ordeal you've been through, most of Hargeisa knows" whispered Sagal. After their chat had ended Abdirahman knew this was the woman he wanted to marry. Her charisma, beauty, and intelligence had him thinking about her for nights ahead. Over the next few months, Abdirahman introduced himself to Sagal's uncle, and the pair began to learn a lot about each other and realised how they had a similar upbringing. After 6 months of their first encounter Abdirahman and Sagal wed, the wedding was a small one with close friends and family attending. The year was now 1977 and Abdirahman had 2 successful businesses and had a beautiful 2-year-old boy named Ali. His family also lived in a beautiful 4-bedroom house in the middle of Hargeisa. It was the holy month of Ramadan and Abdirahman's 2 maids were preparing afur (food to break the fast) for him and his wife. As they prepared the feast, Abdirahman and his family were in their spacious living room, surrounded by their child's laughter. He finally had everything he had ever dreamed of. "I'm sorry Abdirahman, however, one of the maids is not feeling well and needs to be taken home. I can get a replacement maid for the rest of the week" said one of the maids who was named Hodan. Abdirahman agreed as he tucked into his afur, Hodan had also stated that the only way they could get a replacement is from the bus stand where other maids would look for work. "No problem," said Abdirahman. Abdirahman and his wife were finally finished with their afur and presumed to take Ali to bed. After this was done Abdirahman and his wife Sagal asked Hodan to look after Ali while they both went to the masjid to pray Taraweeh (Ramadan night prayer). She had agreed and Abdirahman and his wife both set off to the masjid to pray while Ali was left at the family's home. After they had gone, Hodan went to recruit and came back with a new maid. She showed the new maid around the house and the daily tasks she would undertake in the household while Abdirahman and Sagal were at the masjid. The maids then went to sleep to be ready for work the next morning, Abdirahman and his wife had finally arrived home before suhoor (night meal). And as Abdirahman was keen to go to bed after he had finished his suhoor, he wanted to check up on his beautiful little baby Ali. He then presumed to check on Ali, as he moved closer to Ali's bed, he saw that the bed was empty, and the window was left open. Abdirahman couldn't make sense of this, he then took a closer look at Ali's bed and spotted a red bandana with a note placed next to it on Ali's pillow. Abdirahman's then realised his son had been taken, by the same evil woman who had vowed to take revenge against him.

CHAPTER 7

LOST

"How could this happen?", "Who did this?" shouted Abdirahman, Sagal was shaking in the corner of the room, panicking every second that went past. "The new maid is missing too; I cannot believe this" Hodan cried. "She must've taken Ali while I was asleep," Hodan said. "This cannot be happening" Sagal kept repeating. Hodan awoke to the noise the couple had been causing. "How could you let this happen? our Son has been taken; you were supposed to look after him" Sagal yelled. Abdirahman looked closer at Ali's bed and saw the note with a red bandana next to it, he had realised this was the work of Hooyo Macaan who had disguised herself as the new maid and kidnapped his only son. He thought he had escaped her; However, she had finally come to take revenge on not only him but his family. Abdirahman was now alone in the room, while his wife shouted at the maids, he then proceeded to read the letter.

The letter read the following:

"II waran (How are you) Abdirahman, the reason why I took your child is that you took my grandchild Idil, you led her to those people. That police officer killed her and now you will have to pay for the consequences at hand. Do you want to see your son in one-piece Abdirahman? I'm going to take it as a yes. So, here is what you are going to do bring me the box your father left you. Once you bring this to the caves, I reside in by yourself with the help of no one, you can have your darling Ali back. Also, funny how you named him after my last meal before I saw you. He was a delicious young fellow".

Abdirahman was shocked, how did she manage to find him? How did she know about the box his father had left him before he went, and what did it contain? Dozens of questions surrounded Abdirahman's mind. But he had to be strong as he held back his tears. The police had finally arrived at Abdirahman's household, his wife called Abdirahman to the living room where the two police officers were sitting. "Now Abdirahman, I know how you feel in this time, but we need your cooperation walalo" said the tall skinny police officer as he sipped his tea Hodan had prepared for him. "Do you have any enemies, anyone that wants to hurt you or your family?" said the police officer. Abdirahman sat with his wife, his face turned dull and sad, he whispered "No" in a raspy voice, his voice had turned like that due to the shouting he had been doing after he found out his son had been taken. Abdirahman left the room and went to his bedroom as he planned in his head how he would take his son back. Sagal followed her husband to the bedroom but had trouble sleeping for the first few hours, but then fell into a deep sleep, Abdirahman, however, waited until Sagal was fast asleep and made his way out of the door. He wore his macawiis and white vest and slowly crept outside, while his wife slept unaware of what was going on. He started his truck on that hot summer's night, flashbacks crept into Abdirahman's head. Flashbacks of his father leaving his household when he was just a child. However, he stayed strong and drove to his mother's house, he remembered that he had buried the box one year ago in his mother's front yard. He dug the box up once he had arrived at his mother's house, the whole of Hargeisa was quiet, this was evident due to the sounds the insects were giving off. He had retrieved the box and went back to his truck. As Abdirahman drove out of Hargeisa, he remembered the ordeal and misery he once went through with Sharmarke. However, this was for his son, for what kept him going as he knew he never really knew his father. As Abdirahman's truck went faster and faster, he stopped at the checkpoint in Hargeisa which led towards the mountains which were on the same route to Berbera. The checkpoint officer left his base and saw Abdirahman was travelling alone. "Where are you going warya" the officer said. "Berbera, adeer (uncle) I am a businessman from inner Hargeisa" Abdirahman said as he slid some money into the officer's pocket. The checkpoint opened, and Abdirahman drove into the night, as he drove sunrise was fast approaching and Abdirahman glared at the beauty of the mountains on either side of him. He stopped at the side of the road and proceeded to pray Fajr (prayer) he prayed like it was his last prayer and prayed that his son would come home safe with him. When Abdirahman had finished, he went back into his car and drove quicker as daybreak was approaching. He was getting worried that Hooyo Macaan would start to lose patience, but he couldn't think like that, not now he was so close. He couldn't believe it, he had finally arrived, he saw Hooyo Macaan's checkpoint in the distance. It was a makeshift tree trunk covered in spikes like he remembered when he was kidnapped by Sharmarke and Warsame. Abdirahman slowly drove to the checkpoint and saw a tall skinny man, it was Sharmarke he had lost a lot of weight from when he had last seen him. "Abdirahman? Abdirahman is here, Abdirahman is here with the box!" he repeated. Sharmarke wasn't silenced this time as he opened the checkpoint for Abdirahman, there was a leaver that he pulled as the trunk of the tree rose above the truck as Abdirahman drove into Hooyo Macaan's habitat. He was back to where it all began, back to the nightmares he thought he had crased from his memories. However, something was very different, the number of Hooyo Macaan's hunters had decreased. The hunters were much skinnier and weaker, almost as if they had been starving and without their food. The area was again still surrounded by Hooyo Macaan's hunters all dressed in traditional Somali attire with spears in their right hand. They were happy to see Abdirahman, which confused him as he walked behind Sharmarke up the levels of the mountains grabbing on the box his father had given him, and the box he had so promised to Hooyo Macaan.

CHAPTER 8

THE REUNION

Abdirahman's legs were getting tired, and he started sweating, he was nearly at the top where Hooyo Macaan resided. However, the sound the hunters of Hooyo Macaan were making Abdirahman dizzy, they were humming as Abdirahman climbed each level. "wu yimid, wu yimid (he's here)" Hooyo Macaan's workers kept chanting. Abdirahman realised they were talking about the box, he wondered what this old box contained? Why are they so happy it's finally here? So many questions were left unanswered with Abdirahman as he edged closer to the top. "Waan joogna (we're here)" said Sharmarke. The pair had finally reached the top of the caves, Abdirahman saw the woman who had destroyed his life, she was right in front of his eyes. Sitting with both of her legs stretched out on the floor, smirking as she giggled at Abdirahman. "You were fast, but don't worry Abdirahman your son loves it here we're taking very good care of him," said Hooyo Macaan as Ali sat in her lap fiddling with a leaf Hooyo Macaan had given him. Abdirahman was stuck in an endless stare at the monster who had now kidnapped his only son. "Aren't you going to speak?" Hooyo Macaan said. "Why would you do this? Why me?" shouted Abdirahman. Hooyo

Macaan stood up and came closer to Abdirahman. "Why me?" she repeated sarcastically. "You were never special, Abdirahman, your father, and his friend took something of mine years ago. He and that European man stole my item! And I used you to get it back, you see," said Hooyo Macaan. Abdirahman was in shock, he was always told his father was an officer and worked with the British abroad. "My father? My father died years ago, stop lying to me! He was an officer he didn't steal!" said Abdirahman. "That is what you think Abdirahman, but he sold anything he could find in the countryside with that British man, anything he found you name it he would take and sell, but he stole from the wrong person and that's why he suffered in my hands". Abdirahman was left bemused, Hooyo Macaan had just confessed to killing his father but none of it made sense before he could speak, Hooyo Macaan screamed: "Bring me the prisoner now!". Abdirahman heard the footsteps and the sound of shackles coming up the stairs, there came up an old man of medium height, his beard had touched his chest and his hair had grown considerably big and curly. Abdirahman looked closer and saw that this man had a badge on his shirt, the same one his father used to wear.

"Abdirahman aabo, ii waran (how are you)" the old man said as he stood next to Hooyo Macaan. Abdirahman was in joy as he now knew his father wasn't dead, he was right in front of his very eyes and he was almost certain he could save him from this evil woman. Abdirahman said the following to his father as he stared into his eyes while tears overwhelmed him. "How are you still alive? All this time I thou...". "Shut your mouth, I hear a car!" shouted Hooyo Macaan. One of Hooyo Macaan's soldiers had reported a car had arrived at the premises. "Bring them up here" Hooyo Macaan mumbled in disgust. As the visitors reached the top Abdirahman looked behind his shoulder, he saw his wife walk towards him. Abdirahman was left baffled, how did she find him? How did she know where to look? "You shouldn't be here Sagal, it's dangerous that's why I left you while you were asleep to save our son from these people". Sagal completely ignored Abdirahman as she shed a tear and walked towards Hooyo Macaan in speed. Abdirahman kept shouting at her to stay away from what he called a monster. As Sagal went closer to her, she gave Hooyo Macaan a kiss on the cheek. "Sorry I'm late Ayeeyo (grandma)" said Sagal. "Oh, didn't you know

Abdirahman? Sagal is my granddaughter thank you so much for bringing her home" screamed Hooyo Macaan. Abdirahman dropped the box from his hand in shock; he had been betrayed by his own wife!

PART 2

CHAPTER 9

,

THE PRISON

"Xabsiga geeya imika (take them to prison), they need to learn their lesson again!" yelled Hooyo Macaan, they will learn how to behave there. Abdirahman looked back at what he called his wife, the woman who had cheated him and bore him a child that he thought had an honest mother. He wept in despair as he couldn't believe what the woman, he loved had done to him. "Wait, before you take me and my father to our cells. I want to ask you a question Sagal, why did you do this? why, why, why!?" Sagal looked down and started to giggle, she then looked up at her husband and said "Let me ask you the same question, why did you get my sister killed? Do you remember Idil? She was my world, and I looked up to her all my life. Me and Ayeeyo (grandma) knew you would return to Hargeisa and start a new life. So, what an amazing opportunity for me to mask myself as a new businesswoman in the city. I just knew you would fall for it which is the funny thing in all of this".The whole cave turned quiet and Abdirahman's father could not believe what he was hearing. "I tracked you as you set up shop every morning and even set up shop in front of you on purpose with my uncle who I owe this all too. I knew you would feel sympathy for me when I told you about my grandmother and my very sad sob story of a past, Hooyo Macaan told me you were a sympathetic person and what an amazing trait I could take advantage of," said Sagal. "How could you cheat me like this?" Shouted Abdi "You even married me and bore me a child, what about our child? How could you do this! How will we explain this to him when he's older?" "Well Abdirahman, you won't be in his life anymore after ayeeyo is done with you, and when you are gone from our lives, I'll raise him to be part of our group of hunters to continue our ancient trade", smiled Sagal. As the sun nearly set on the cave, Hooyo Macaan then spoke: "Ok that's enough catching up now, take them to the cells and make sure your husband never leaves just like his father". As Abdirahman and his father were about to follow Sharmarke down to the cells, Hooyo Macaan grabbed his shoulder and told him to look at her. "You won't be leaving like the last time I put you in the caves. This time I will imprison you in my high-security cells behind the caves. The same place I stored your father for all these years, so please don't even think of escaping because there will be dire consequences Abdirahman". Abdirahman and his father followed Sharmarke to Hooyo Macaan's prison. They made their way down the steps and onto the ground, as they walked to the prison Sharmarke told Abdirahman that he won't be escaping this time repeating the words "ma baxsan kartid (you won't escape)", the journey to the prison was a five-minute walk from the caves and the group finally arrived. Abdirahman looked up, and the prison was large, walls covered all corners of the prison which was around 100 square feet of dry ground. Watchers could be seen from the top of the prison rooftops just in case anyone tried to make an escape. Sharmarke dropped the two at the gates of the prison and a short guard around 5ft tall who had a dark complexion with long curly hair approached Abdirahman and his father, he was carrying a long sharp spear and was covered in the traditional white Somali cloak. "Now listen here,", he said as he spoke with a stutter. "My name is Dacawo (Fox), and every corner of these walls are controlled by me and myself only with the help of these useless guards you see around you. You need to understand be on your best behaviour and maybe we'll let you roam the playground for an extra hour every day, what I mean is to be on your best behaviour and you won't be killed. However, if you try to escape Abdirahman, just remember the consequences will be very very bad!". Dacawo then ordered his guards to open the gates to the prison and Abdirahman and his father made their way inside the walls. The prison had 12 cells and each cell holding 4 prisoners; the prison was also split across two wings the right-wing and the left-wing. The pair then followed Dacawo into the prison and as they made their way in, Abdirahman had realised there would be no escape from these walls.

CHAPTER 10

LOCKED AWAY

The ground was rock hard and hot, and the place was roaming with guards, as they walked further into the prison the right and left-winged cells were filled with innocent prisoners all staring at Abdirahman and his father from either side. When they had finally arrived, Abdirahman was presented with a large caged like cell where the barriers had become old and rusty. As Dacawo opened the cell door, the pair were ordered inside then the cell doors were finally closed on the pair, Dacawo uttered a final statement before he left "get comfortable in there Abdirahman because you're never leaving". Abdirahman and his father looked behind them and saw three other prisoners sitting down behind them on the floor. The first of them was an Arab man with a fat body and long curly hair which reached his earlobe, his beard had grown scruffy and his white shirt and brown trousers had become dirty and sandy as he sat in the corner of the cell, Abdirahman was surprised at first to find a non-Somali man in the prison, a majority of the Arabs were traders but then Abdirahman slowly realised he must have been fooled while doing business with Hooyo Macaan's hunters.

Abdirahman then looked to the other corner of the cell and saw a tall man kneeling down and inspecting the floor of the cells with a small cadey (toothbrush), the man was dark in complexion and had short hair as if he had cut it recently and he also had a long goatee stretching to the higher part of his throat. The man looked like he was in his early 30s and he kept whispering to himself as he continued to inspect the floor. Abdirahman's father sat on the other corner of the cell near the door and watched the guards, he knew he would live the rest of his days out in the cells, his eyes had turned red and he was tired, however, he wouldn't sleep as he continued to look on at the prison. The prison was quiet as the other prisoners in the other cells had given up hope of ever leaving due to the high security. Abdirahman did not bother disturbing his father, instead he had a flashback to the caves he was in with his late friend Ali and could still hear his screams in his head. The two men reminded him of Ali, but if it wasn't for Ali's sacrifice, Abdirahman would never have made the first escape. "What are your names?" Said Abdirahman. The Arab man cleared his throat and began to speak. "My name's Adam brother, your name is Abdirahman, right? You are Nasir's son?". "Yes, I am".

Said Abdirahman. "Nice to meet you," said Adam. Abdirahman was still surprised as to why an Arab man ended up in a prison-like this, he then asked him how he ended up in this cell. Adam then cleared his throat once more and started to tell his story. "I was born and raised in Aden (South Yemen) to a very wealthy family with quite a lot of land and livestock. My father was a member of the government and my mother was a doctor. As a child I was not very good in school, I never used to pay attention in class and I used to think everything would be set out for me, oh how I was wrong. When I was a child, my father had plans for me to study politics in the university and one day be like him. A member of the parliament or maybe even the president, however, I became a disappointment to my parents. When I reached high school, I continued my ways of not turning up to class and not paying attention. I'll be totally honest with you I did not care about politics I just wanted to have fun. When I finished high school, I went home and broke the news to my father that I never made it to higher education. I remember that day it was one of the hottest days of the year and the heat did not help cool down my father's anger with me. He couldn't even look me in the eyes when I told him the news, however, he was my father, and he had other plans for me when it was apparent that I would never work for the government as he did. We had business with trading livestock with the Somali republic and my father put me in charge of this when I was sent to the port of Aden. 5 weeks ago at the port, I met a Somali man named Sharmarke, he told me he had an amazing deal for me. He offered to sell me his land in this very area we are in now, the deal sounded amazing and I asked him to continue speaking about this piece of land. The price of the land was cheap, and he told me he needed to sell it quickly as he wanted to move to Nairobi and start a new life. I agreed and crossed the sea and headed to the Somali Republic, when I arrived in Berbera, I realised how beautiful the country was and couldn't wait to buy the land Sharmarke was telling me about. As we drove to Hargeisa, he told me stories of how he had extra livestock for me as part of the deal which excited me even further. Sharmarke then offered me some water and before I knew it I fell fast asleep for several hours, I then woke up and realised he set me up, I felt weak and helpless as he took me here to Hooyo Macaan. As petrified as I was, I kept quiet and regretted not letting my father know I went across the sea to this country.

When I followed Sharmarke to the caves he told me I would be devoured by Hooyo Macaan, this was someone I trusted, however, I accepted my fate". Abdirahman felt like he was hearing the same story he went through the first time he was captured by Sharmarke; it was as if they plan this in a recurring pattern always aiming for traders in the city or close by. Adam then continued his story of how he was captured. "When Sharmarke took me to Hooyo Macaan she ordered him to take me to the prisons,

I was shocked at first, but she insisted she did not want to eat me, instead she wanted to use me as her labourer in the land on the prison. And that is how I ended up here Abdirahman, and therefore you're here now as a worker for her for life." Abdirahman stayed quiet for a while and then said: "no we are escaping, this isn't life this isn't how we should be living I need to leave and go back to my mother, I came here for my child and I am not leaving without him".

"Listen walalo, I've been here for 1 year and every time I think about breaking out I realise it will be an impossible task," said the other man across the cell as he continued marking the floor with his toothbrush in an up and down motion.

CHAPTER 11

THE MYSTERIOUS MAN

Abdirahman asked the man who he was and then the man continued to speak "I'm from Las Canood and the only reason I am here is to break my father out, my mother always told me about him being a traveller across the plains of Woqooyi Galbeed (north-west Somali Region), when I was 8 he left us to work in Djibouti and never returned, no words were ever heard from him again. Growing up, it was just myself and my mother until she remarried 3 years after my father left and my new stepfather didn't even acknowledge my existence. However, he was the only person we could rely on as my mother and I was struggling. Domestic abuse was common from him and it got worse and worse as years went by, bruises and marks were common sites on my mother's face and I even fell victim to him. On my 14th birthday, I returned home from school and that was the day I would never forget, I found my mother's body on the floor of my bedroom and marks to her head could be seen. I broke down and felt faint, what makes it worse was her husband who committed this act fled the scene and never returned. I blame myself every day, every single night I think what if I stayed home from school?". "Stop right there young man, everything is qadr Allah (written by Allah) don't think like this," said Nasir. "That's true however I vow to take my revenge against him, and the thing is I will find him one day he will never escape me," said the man. "How did you manage to get in here, and by the way what is your name?" Abdirahman asked. "My name is Fosi brother, and I did not end up in here like anyone of you. Warsame brought me here as I managed to strike a deal with him when I reached Hargeisa.". Abdirahman then Shouted at Fosi and told him that he shouldn't trust Warsame as he was one of the first people to kidnap him and take him to Hooyo Macaan. "No brother, he was the only option I had to come to this prison, Warsame met me in Hargeisa after a friend of mine told me he knew where missing people ended up that travelled around this region, hoping that he would have any information on my father. He told me he heard of his name in the caves and after befriending him through trade he told me about Hooyo Macaan. He told me about the prisons and the caves too, you need to understand he is a slave to Hooyo Macaan. She has his brother in here and to keep him alive he does everything she says. After weeks of asking him the whereabouts of these caves, we finally struck a deal, I would break his brother out too if he would lead me to the caves and we made our way here. When we arrived at the location, it was a peak year of feasting for Hooyo Macaan and she needed workers. This then finally led me here to this prison". The group descended into an argument after Fosi discussed his horrific life story, Nasir wanted to stay and not risk his life or his son's life again especially the final warning which was given to them by Dacawo and Hooyo Macaan. He was in prison for years and knew the consequences that would come if they were ever to get caught again. Adam also disagreed and was happy and comfortable in the cell, he kept telling the group his father would travel from Yemen one day and break him out. But he was the least enthusiastic and most cowardice of the group which was obvious. Every time Fosi would tell him a plan of escaping he would crawl into a ball and put his hands over his ears. As Abdirahman sat on the floor he started to think, he had just met Fosi and escaping with him would be a big risk, especially with Fosi planning the escape instead of himself. He wasn't sure if he could trust him with his life, especially with the way Hooyo Macaan had threatened him. But Abdirahman knew he was the only person who could help him escape.

"I'm with you on this Fosi, anything you need me to do to help let me know," he said. "To go through with this Abdirahman, I need your father and Adam on board too," said Fosi. Abdirahman looked at his father who was still sitting on the floor of the cell, daydreaming. He begged his father and tried to persuade him that they all needed to escape together, until Nasir finally spoke "I tried to escape once you know, years ago I pickpocketed one of the guards while he lay asleep near my cell, I unlocked the door and tried to escape the prison. Hooyo Macaan caught me trying to escape and tortured me for days, not only did she torture me, but my cellmate was executed as a lesson for my mistake, do you want the same to happen to you my son?

"You've already been dead for years Aabo (Dad) our family accepted your death for years and sitting in this cell and not doing anything about it will guarantee that we'll die in this cell. Remember what you taught me Aabo, about having belief and trust in Allah.

Furthermore, I don't want my son growing up without a father the way I did. So please Aabo let us escape and start fresh and let us all put our trust in the most high".

Nasir got up from where he was sitting and realised that after all those years, he had been in this cell he forgot the most important thing he had told his son before he left, putting his trust in Allah and fighting for his freedom. "When do we start the escape" he whispered, as he hugged his son.

Abdirahman then proceeded to go to the other side of the cell to Adam and spoke to him gently while Adam crawled up into a ball as if he was trying to block out the ideas from the other men. "Listen, Adam, you're a very smart man and you have your whole life ahead of you.

Who else could say they've escaped a prison in Africa when you return to Yemen and think about it you will be treated as a hero from your people and, more importantly, your father"?

CHAPTER 12

PRAYER

Adam then slowly got up and told Fosi he was ready to escape, while he shed a tear, he knew he needed to get back to his father in Yemen. The three men now spread out in each corner of the cell; they had finally agreed on one thing, which was to escape from Hooyo Macaan's hell hole. They were now determined to get back to their lives, and Abdirahman was more determined than ever to free his father from these ruins. Abdirahman then went over to Fosi who had been repeating his routine of scratching the floor with his cadey (wooden toothbrush) all while sweat was dripping from his face. "Fosi, I was meaning to ask you where is your father? I mean what cell is he in?". Fosi then looked up at Abdirahman "I don't know which cell he's in Abdirahman, I don't know" he sighed as he went back to circling the floor with his toothbrush. Abdirahman then looked down at Fosi in confusion "What do you mean you don't know what cell he is in, isn't that the main reason you're in the prison?". "Listen to me Abdirahman, you can trust me, Warsame said once we figure a way out of the cells, he will tell me the cell my father's in. So, we will have to just wait until the night before". "What do you mean you don't know which cell he's in, I told you never to trust

Warsame, He will trick you and deceive you Fosi I know this man and when he leaves you in the dirt, how are we going to get out of this mess" whispered Abdirahman. Fosi breathed in and out he got up and looked Abdirahman in the face, as the two men stared at each other Fosi realised they were of similar height. Abdirahman also reminded Fosi of a younger version of himself as they continued to look at each other. "Listen Abdirahman, put your trust in Allah and remember we will get out of this mess you speak of, but I can't tell you the plan until tomorrow night so let us get some rest". Night had broken on the prison and as Dacawo roamed around the prison yard, he walked towards the cell of the three men with his small frame as he carried a large leather mat in his hand. He opened the cell door and threw the mat at Abdirahman's face as he lay in his corner. "Sleep with this it will keep you extra warm for your stay warya" he stuttered. As he walked out of the cell Fosi stared at Dacawo's hands getting a glimpse of the keys he had used to open all the cells, Dacawo looked back and came closer to Fosi grabbing his hair and said.

"Look closely at my keys warya because this is the closest you will ever get to freedom". The small man then walked away chuckling to himself as his guards closed the doors of the cell. The three men all lay in each corner of the room with their leather mats covered in sweat due to the heat, and the smell of the hole (toilet) spread throughout the cell as Adam used it to relieve himself. Abdirahman lived a pretty tough life growing up; however, he thought to himself nothing compared to the squalor and unhygienic conditions these cells were in. As Abdirahman lay in his corner that very night he realised Fosi was still awake, staring at the gates of the prison doors on the outside all while whispering "waan soo socdaa". When the sun had risen on the prison, the men prayed the morning prayer (Fajr) and the prison guards laughed and mocked them while they prayed. Life was repetitive for the next few weeks, Abdirahman asking Fosi how they would get out of the prisons. Nasir still on the corner of his cell thinking and twirling his hair. Adam kept to himself in his corner, praying he would see his father again. Many weeks had passed now and Abdirahman grew frustrated, he had lost a considerable amount of weight and Fosi still wouldn't tell him the plan of their escape; he was slowly losing hope.

CHAPTER 13

THE 24th OF JULY

As Abdirahman was about to speak with Fosi about the escape, the prison doors opened, and a familiar face came through the doors of the prison. The man walked behind Dacawo and they slowly came towards the cell of the men, the mysterious man was hooded in black and grabbed onto the bars of the cell and took off his hood. "Salam alaykum, the man said to the already lost prisoners". Abdirahman looked up and realised it was Warsame, however, he didn't greet Warsame back remembering everything he had done to him in the past. "Wake up Fosi someone is here for you," said Abdirahman as he patted Fosi on the back while he lay asleep. Fosi quickly got up and went to the cell to speak with Warsame, "let me speak to this disgusting prisoner Dacawo, he owes me some information for a few potential targets for Hooyo Macaan's next victims" said Warsame. Dacawo agreed to leave the premises giggling and dribbling as he walked away in the dusty playground which lay in the middle of the prison. "Listen to me carefully Fosi and do not forget this date 24/7" whispered Warsame straight into Fosi's ear. He looked at his face and walked away out of the prison gate as if he had taken a major risk. Fosi looked at Abdirahman and smiled, this was odd as Fosi hadn't smiled since Abdirahman had arrived in his cell. "Why are you smiling"? asked Nasir, as he lay on the floor, chewing on a toothpick. Fosi didn't say a word until night had fallen on the prison and Dacawo had left the prison gates, as the group waited for Fosi to speak they finally heard the following words utter from his mouth. "Come towards me brothers". "Warsame has given me the date, the date of what? you might ask, however, the 24th of July is the night we will be escaping". "The 24th of July is in 2 days! how do you expect us to prepare in 2 days you crazy man" whispered Adam. Abdirahman and his father looked at each other, and they both agreed with Adam as 2 days felt like such a short amount of time to plan an escape. Fosi sighed and told them to give him a chance to explain. "Listen to me in 2 days there will be a total eclipse which will cause darkness. For hundreds of years, Hooyo Macaan and her people have fled to the caves and do not come out until the solar eclipse has ended. No one knows why they do it however ancient myths have stated that Hooyo Macaan's ancestors were royals throughout these lands, one day there was a drought and the royal family was blamed for not providing enough resources to help the slowly starving population. The citizens then banished the royal family from their original villages on a night which was a solar eclipse and the caves were where they had gone first. And for hundreds of years, the lost royals were never to be seen again until they found us". Nasir crept closer and asked Fosi what this meant for their escape and how it would help them in any way shape or form.

"You need to understand they all go to their caves on the night of the eclipse, so that will be our chance to finally escape this hell hole, however ,we can only do this with a special plan of mine which I cannot share with any of you in this given time so trust me" sighed Fosi. "Listen Fosi, this sounds like an amazing idea but you're forgetting one thing, how will we escape in total darkness. Please, we need to think this through" complained Adam as he felt almost faint from the idea. Fosi then put his hand on Adam's shoulder, "listen to me carefully brother, I will tell you how we are getting out. Everyone listen carefully as we only have two days to plan this".

CHAPTER 14

THE LISTENERS

The group then huddled together in the blistering heat as they tried avoiding attention from the guards watching from the yard in the middle of the prison. "Now listen here everyone, we have tomorrow which is the 23rd and after tomorrow which will be the 24th. We have 4 missions which I have spread between those two days; those 4 missions will involve two items we will need to escape the prison. The first mission is to get the pills the guards give the prisoners when they go on hunger strikes to make them fall asleep, they normally force-feed them the pills and then force-feed them their food. These pills are not like normal sleeping pills, they are extremely powerful and were designed by one of Hooyo Macaan's scientists. They cause a person to sleep for 4 – 6 hours without waking up once. A new batch will be delivered tomorrow and given to Dacawo while they put us to work on the yard outside our cell so be ready,". Abdirahman was confused and asked, "Why do we need pills Fosi?". "Brother, this will all make sense on the day of the escape, so have sabr Abdirahman please," Fosi replied. After Fosi was interrupted by Abdirahman he continued discussing the plan. "Moreover, brothers after we have done our yard work, we will need to get the most important person into this cell. And that is Warsame's brother Cawaale he was once in this cell one year ago; however, the guards moved him to make space for Adam. But I have a plan to bring him in here". The group then asked Fosi how it would be possible to bring another prisoner into their cell. "A few weeks ago, Cawaale was sentenced to death by Hooyo Macaan. The date is set for the night of the 25th of July at midnight. Every prisoner has one last request before they are executed a few days before and I will need to tell Cawaale to request he sleeps in this cell one last time by giving him a note on the 23rd of July,". Adam asked Fosi why Cawaale who was such a young adolescent was sentenced to be killed. "Brothers, Cawaale was responsible for smuggling food from the outside while working with one of the guards. That gave Hooyo Macaan the excuse to kill the guard and sentence Cawaale to death. Why doesn't she kill him now? You might ask, however, it's because she wants to use him for the big yard clean-up tomorrow. The more the people the stronger they'll be.". "And what is the 3rd task?" Nasir said all while he struggled to speak due to the heat, his blue shirt had become soaked in sweat. "The third mission my brothers will be tough; however, it is the reason Abdirahman made his way to this location in the first place and that is saving his son,". Abdirahman shed a small tear as Fosi said this, he had arrived at the prison to save his son and found his father was also here too this made him ready to give everything to save the both of them. "The final mission brothers will be the most important of them all, freeing my father from this prison. The whole prison turned quiet, Fosi realised years had passed and Warsame still hadn't told Fosi where his father was being held. For the first time in years, he was worried.

Abdirahman was about to speak on the matter, however, stayed quiet as he knew the response Fosi would give him. Nasir then responded to Fosi still tired from the years he had endured in the cell. "Listen here, brother, I've tried escaping once before and it did not go well. However, the plan you have told me maybe the best I've heard in all my years.

But say we escape brother what is the point? Hooyo Macaan will send her dhego (listeners) on us who are based in every city in Somalia and across East Africa and beyond,".

Adam and Abdirahman looked at each other while the experienced men conversed. They knew in their minds what they were both thinking, that Abdirahman's father was telling the truth.

They had endured so much heartache, and Abdirahman had escaped before but what was the point in escaping again? What was the point of freeing all these men if Hooyo Macaan would make her return? While the two younger men continued to look and almost read each other's thoughts.

Abdirahman's father continued to speak "now Fosi your plan is amazing as such, getting the pills, bringing Cawaale to this cell, freeing my grandson and then your father. However, we need to defeat Hooyo Macaan, and I have the solution to this problem and the solution is in the box my son was carrying.

CHAPTER 15

THE TWINS

Adam and Fosi both looked confused to what this box was and asked Nasir what was in it. Nasir then cleared his throat and before telling them about the box, he looked the young men in their eyes and asked them to swear never to tell anyone about the contents of this box. The three men all swore to Allah never to tell a soul, Nasir then continued to speak after they had sworn. "Abdirahman growing up I believe your mother told you I was a soldier during the 30s and 40s fighting in world war 2 and a seaman during the 50s, part of this is true my son however not all of it. Growing up in Hargeisa during the British rule was quite an interesting one, I was born in 1918 and my father fought with the British during the start of the 20th century and sadly died and my brothers and sisters were looked after by my mother on her own. My mother was a midwife in the hospital during this time too, and alhamdullilah I had the chance to finish high school. My main aim was to fly over to Britain and studying at the University of Oxford, imagine that a young Somali boy, getting into Oxford. I had excelled in both education and physical training with the army, one officer had realised my potential in training and in my educational abilities. He then offered me a chance to go to Oxford and also be part of their military program and research team when I had graduated. When I graduated from high school, the officer covered the expenses of my fees and flight to Britain and made sure my mother and siblings were looked after when I was away. When I arrived in Britain, the customs were very different, and I studied with many important figures that are in the world today. I was lucky, however, as English was taught in most schools growing up in Hargeisa the language barrier did not affect me one bit. The country itself was very much different as you assume the weather was much different and getting used to the cold and rain was difficult especially during military training. However, I made many friends from across the world and the experience was unmatched. When I graduated, the promise I made to the officer was to be kept, and I joined the British army in their base within British Somaliland. When I arrived in Hargeisa, I was taken to their base accompanied by the officer whose name was officer Stevens and his commander officer Williams who was a very harsh and greedy man. After arriving back in Hargeisa from Britain I didn't even have the chance to stay with my mother after all my years in the U.K., instead, officer Williams said we must make our way to the twins. The twins were known to the British as the mountains just outside Hargeisa which were known to us as Naaso Hablood, these mountains were named this due to the resemblance of breasts. We then hopped into officer William's truck and made our way to Naaso Hablood, I started to ask questions to officer Stevens about why we were not staying at the main base in Hargeisa. However, he told me not to ask those types of questions, especially in front of the commander. It was 1942 at the time and the world was still at war but the commander had other priorities rather than prepare. We finally arrived at the mountains and officer Williams took an unusual turn underneath a gap in between the two mountains which had newly built roads. The roads led well beneath the mountains and signs which were produced in the U.K. could be seen on either side; The area had a few camps and when we made our way into one of them, twins named Ahmed and Mustafa came across us. They were both tall and skinny, both were wearing long black cloaks and goggles made from plastic. Ahmed had long curly hair while Mustafa had short hair with a scar on his right cheek. I was very surprised at the site of the two men, scientists out in the middle of nowhere who were also Somali too baffled me. The commander went over to speak to Ahmed and kept saying, 'Have we found it warya, have we found it?'. I was confused and was not ready to ask what they were looking for as I was still shocked at why we were taken to a research camp instead of an army base. Ahmed And Mustafa then told us to follow them, their cloaks were rubbing against the sand and officer Williams who had gone red due to the heat, led us behind Ahmed while he walked with his short frame and bright blonde hair. Ahmed took us to the second camp which was the size of a large tent and inside was something amazing. There were large machines and equipment used to dig up mountains for minerals. The tent was covered in drills and tracking equipment. 'What is this, why aren't we at the army camp?' I asked the 4 other men. They all looked at me and started to smile, 'listen to me you little boy I am not here to fight a stupid war I am here for my own gain you see' Commander Williams told me. I then knew that the commander would use me for his own personal financial gain, as well as the use of officer Stevens who had no say in any of this. The commander and Ahmed then continued their search within the confinements of the tent, Ahmed would be waiting for any signals from his machine which searched the area to alert him once this secretive item or items were found. Ahmed then said, 'I have been here 4 weeks commander and the box is nowhere to be found, I think we should just leave'.

CHAPTER 16

GREED

However, the commander did not like anything Ahmed was saying and kept telling him to look harder. The commander's greediness had caused him to use the war as a means of gaining his own wealth and to use my training and education I was provided in the U.K. for himself. I was extremely confused as to why the commander was after a box. Mustafa's scar started to give me doubts about how he obtained them, they didn't look like they were caused by a knife or an accident and it looked like he had been scratched. Mustafa kept sweating as the commander and Ahmed spoke; However, he finally uttered the words which made the commander a very happy man. 'Commander, my brother's lying to you, we found the box in the caves near Laas geel. Laas Geel's an old site with paintings dating back thousands of years; however, they are not empty. Our machines led us to those caves and alerted us that the stones were there. So, we went looking and as we entered the caves, we found them in a room at the very top floor which looked like it was already inhabited by someone. The leather bedsheet on the floor and pieces of rope and food took over the room. As we were about to take the box, we were greeted by a very large woman who was hideous to look at. She was wearing a red bandana and had a long dress which stretched to the floor and she gave us a chance to leave unharmed, however, I did not accept this even though my brother told us that we should leave. I was attacked by her; luckily, we made the escape out of there. Now after witnessing that, I never want to return there, and I never want to risk my life for this box'. My whole life then changed forever when the commander looked Mustafa in his eyes, took out his pistol, and shot him through the head. He threatened all of us and said if we didn't comply with his plan then we would be next, we continued to watch the horror in Ahmed's face as the murder unfolded in front of our very eyes and we were forced to follow his orders from then on. Ahmed then had the gun to his head and I and officer Stevens watched in shock as the last remaining twin was forced to speak about the whereabouts of the box. Ahmed took a deep breath while tears rolled down his face, he had just lost his brother and he could barely let the words roll off his tongue. The caves are in Laas Geel; however, it is inhabited by a woman, a large woman who fears no one. 'The only reason she let us live was to tell the story of who she is, and she will not let that box out of her site'.

Ahmed then suddenly stopped speaking as officer Williams let his last bullet enter Ahmed's skull leaving him in cold blood within the hot and steamy laboratory. He looked at me and officer Stevens again and said "looks like we're paying a visit to this woman" cackling while he looked on at the mess he left behind. The twins were left in the laboratory while their trackers and machines continued to beep and make noise, the three of us left and I was made to drive the truck while officer Stevens accompanied us in the back. Officer Williams forced me to drive him to Laas Geel all while saying that was the only reason, I was with them, nothing more than a map to get him what he wanted. As we drove to laas geel I could see officer Stevens half asleep in the back, I knew he wasn't the same as officer Williams he was more sympathetic in this situation. Even when we were leaving the laboratory, he told me not to worry and that everything would be fine. I could tell he had enough of taking the crazy blonde man's orders anymore. Officer Williams continued to point the gun to my head as I drove the three of us to officer William's treasured location.

We arrived at the caves in laas geel with no one in sight, it felt as if the twins were telling us a very big lie, but it didn't make sense they literally died for this so why would they lie. Officer Williams then cleared his throat as he continued to direct the gun and walk towards the caves. The caves were much different to how they are now, no checkpoints no spikes or guards it was completely empty and very creepy. We walked up to the cave's, stairs leading us to the very top as we sweated in the blistering heat, we continued to walk up and it started to get dark and the three of us began to feel tired however we made it to the very top of the cave just in time. We saw a room just as the twins described, a blanket was left on the floor and a rope right beside it, the room was covered with small pots and stones.

Officer William's eyes opened wide as he was lost for words, at the end of the room we saw a small box the size of a grown man's wrist polished and shiny placed on top of a small compartment in the ceiling. Officer Williams dropped his gun on the floor and his eyes locked onto the box, he almost looked hypnotized from the angle I was standing in.

He moved ever so closer to that box, and as he moved closer to that box, he was not aware of his surroundings. Officer Williams decided to climb the wall grabbing onto any piece of rock that he could find which would help him steal the box. It took him roughly half an hour to climb the wall and when he finally came to the compartment he smashed the glass and there it was, in his hands had finally held the box, he looked at the box and tried to open it however it wouldn't open.

CHAPTER 17

THE WOMAN

No keyhole, no secret passcode, however, officer Williams didn't care. He finally got what he wanted. He forced me and officer Stevens to help him down while his hands were full; we headed towards him and he threw the box down from where he was so he would have a chance to climb down. Once we were handed the box, we made our way back to the exit to give officer Williams space to dropdown. I thought it was completely wrong, stealing from someone else especially a box that none of us, not even officer Williams would know what was in, but again it was greed that made him take it. It was a gamble, and he put everything he could on that box, he made his way down and as I stared at the box, I could now see why officer Williams was in awe. It was the most beautiful item I had ever seen, and whatever was in this box would have to be very important as the beauty of the box made sure of this. While I looked on at the box, I was pushed onto the floor by officer Stevens whispering to me to get down, he told me to be quiet however I was baffled as to what was happening. We slowly put our heads up behind the entrance of the stairs and saw Hooyo Macaan grab officer Williams and pin him to the wall, 'where is my box, where is it?' she screamed but she didn't wait and slowly bit his neck, I looked away as I heard his screams spread throughout the caves. As she devoured him, she looked in our direction and locked eyes with me, I'll never forget that moment, she didn't care for us, but it almost looked like she knew she would be back for us in the future. She smiled as she stared at me and continued to finish off officer Williams, me and officer Stevens ran for our lives as we made our way down the stairs, we saw the truck and quickly made our way inside however something was missing. We had the box, but we didn't have the keys to the truck. Officer Stevens quickly tried to hot-wire the car, but the heat and pressure didn't make it easy. We could see Hooyo Macaan in the distance running as fast as she could with the blood of officer Williams across her face. However, as she came closer to the car door, the car finally turned on, and we started to move until I felt someone's hand grab my arm from the window. It was the woman we all feared to face Hooyo Macaan. She held onto my arm; However, Officer Stevens swerved the car left and right to make her drop. Her eyes Locked onto both of us as she screamed 'stop you have my box, stop now' she continued to scream and laugh as I tried my best to remove her hand from my arm, however, she was very strong and powerful. As the truck moved left to right she finally gave up and slipped from my arm leaving me with a large scar. She lay on the floor crawling towards us however we were long gone from her terror. Officer Stevens couldn't believe what had happened, we tried to come to terms with the commander's death but couldn't believe what we had just witnessed, a cannibal woman living in the caves had shocked us. As we drove, I twisted the box left and right and it finally opened, as I looked inside, I could see a piece of goat's skin and some writing on it. I read the contents of the box and I was shocked, not because the box didn't contain a special mineral or a rock but something completely different. It contained a map with co-ordinates on the bottom left, the map was dirty and sandy and at the back of it, it read 'saaxib ahay ii caawiya (the friends that help me)' I was confused as to what that meant. Officer Stevens and I continued our travel back to Hargeisa, on our way there I then asked officer Williams what the phrase at the back of the map meant and he thought about it as he drove. Maybe Nasir, maybe it means she has more friends in the co-ordinates she gave at the back of the map. That's when I started to realise what the phrase symbolised, it was a code for the friends and hunters she had in different locations across British protectorate of Somaliland. Ten different locations were shown on the map and 10 different names for Hooyo Macaan's hunters, after what we saw me and officer Stevens had to do something about this problem, as we drove officer Stevens asked me what the first location said. It read Laas canood and as we approached Hargeisa officer Stevens skipped the city and headed straight to Laas canood to wipe out the first of many of Hooyo Macaan's hunters. Over the next 15 years, that was our job going from city to city and hunting down these enemies and I'll tell you this, it wasn't easy at all. So that was my job, not a seaman not a soldier for the British but to defeat these enemies from our people". The whole prison stayed quiet for a few minutes after Nasir had finished his story, he then sighed and said "officer Stevens was killed by Hooyo Macaan. After our car capsized in the desert, we tried to hunt her down and kill her, every day I think about what he did and the way he helped me, he even uttered the shahada with his last breath before he was taken. We managed to defeat 7 out of the 10 hunters and we were so close I tell you". Nasir then went to his corner and told everyone he was ready for the days ahead as he lay on his mat while his eyes stay wide open.

CHAPTER 18

CAWAALE

The next morning came, and the group were made to wake up by force to the sound of dogs barking right outside their cell doors. "Wake up right now all of you, you have to all work now get up" yelled Dacawo as he flung open the door and forced the group out one by one. The group were given pitchforks and forced to dig the ground for Hooyo Macaan to plant her vegetables for her feast. The eclipse was only a day away, and the group dug in the heat for a few hours and then they realised the guards started to get tired in the sun. The guards then started to take shelter underneath the trees while the rest of the inmates continued to dig, Dacawo left the premises and ordered the three remaining guards to keep watch as the inmates continued their work. As they continued to work, Warsame's brother could be seen opposite them on the other side with his back towards the three men. As the guards continued to sleep, Fosi slowly grabbed the note that he had from his back pocket and slowly made his way across to Cawaale who continued to dig on the other side of his cell. He slowly made his way across while clutching onto the note that would guarantee the freedom of his friends and family, he tapped Cawaale on the back and said, "read this tonight before you sleep" and quickly tucked this into Cawaale's back pocket. Cawaale was a stocky man who was of medium height, short hair and had light brown skin, he was sweating due to the heat of the sun and the harsh working conditions him and his wing were put in. However, he was a clever young man and did not look back once while Fosi whispered into his ear. Fosi did not stay too long with Cawaale and quickly went back to his position that he briefly left. The time was now approximately 15:00 pm, and the group had given it their all on both wings. The ground was dug beautifully and ready for Hooyo Macaan to plant her seeds for the vegetables to grow for the coming year. However, Fosi was agitated and anxious as were the other men, this was because they had forgotten one of the most important tasks which was to get the sleeping pills that Fosi desperately needed for the night of the escape. The delivery did not come that day and the stress of the men could be felt throughout the prison; the time was finally up and it was time for the men to go back to their cells bearing in mind that it would be another year before yard work. As the men sat in their cell, they all stayed quiet, the pills were very important for the escape and Fosi kept thinking about how he would get them before tomorrow night's escape. "Fosi come on my friend it can't be that important, you could think of something else for the escape, the sleeping pills seem like something pretty bizarre," said Abdirahman. Fosi stayed quiet as he was not the type to get into an argument or make someone else look stupid. The sun slowly started to set and Fosi was getting impatient as he kept thinking and praying that those sleeping pills would somehow end up in their cell before the escape. Suddenly the cell door opened, Dacawo pushed a young man into the cell and then closed it shouting, "enjoy your last nights with your friends you nacas (fool)". Cawaale slowly got up from the ground and gave Fosi a big hug and thanked him continuously. "Fosi I can't thank you any more than this you are a genius; I was about to be killed and you have saved me from this thank you so much walalo (brother)" cried Cawaale. Fosi stood there and as Cawaale hugged him he continued to think about the task he so miserably failed in. He could not stop blaming himself as Nasir, Adam, and Abdirahman continued to look at the man they put their trust in. "Let's all go to sleep," said Fosi, we have a very long day ahead of us tomorrow and we will need all the rest that we can get.

CHAPTER 19

SILENCE

The group slept and everyone thought about their families and if tomorrow night would be the start of when they would first see them again. Nasir slept and lay there thinking about everything he had been through, but only cared for his son and grandson's safety and knew he would do anything for them. The men lay in their positions nervously that night, and hardly any of them slept much as they continued to wake up and fall back asleep throughout the night. Fajr broke that day and the men all got up each one waiting for the other one to make their Wudu (wash for prayer) and finally congregating in prayer, the birds chirped, and the men finished their prayer. They sat and prayed constantly for Allah to make their escape easy and calm. They didn't go back to sleep and started to converse amongst themselves about what they were to do when they escape. Abdirahman smiled and said, "I cannot wait to take my son back to his grandmother and his uncle, I believe he misses them as much as I do". The group were both nervous and excited at the same time because the day was the 24th of July and after weeks of preparation, the day had finally come to escape the hell hole Hooyo Macaan had put them through. "I cannot wait to have a hero's welcome in

Yemen, my father will probably tell the media and our family members about the survival I had gone through in a foreign country. This will be the route to my father finally trusting me" said Adam. Nasir was repeating a dua (prayer) as he did every day. Fosi and Cawaale spoke with each other about how Fosi's father wouldn't be able to comprehend at how he had orchestrated this plan and would finally be able to meet him on the outside. "My brother comes to visit my cell quite a lot, and your father's doing fine says Warsame, he says he cannot wait to meet you and that there is a whole family that you have no idea about on the outside," said Cawaale. Fosi responded and said he wouldn't be able to wait for the day he meets his extended family on his father's side after the escape. As the group continued to wait, Fosi continued to think about how he would get the sleeping pills from Dacawo. As he thought about it, the prison doors suddenly opened and Dacawo came in with boxes of food and medicine which included the sleeping pills. Fosi's eyes lit up as he saw the boxes, that was the key to the escape but how he would get it was beyond him.

Dacawo would normally go to the cells on the other wing to distribute both food and medicine if needed, however, medicine was normally given to the prisoners who needed it. The sleeping pills were at such a minimum only those who required it was given the pills.

Dacawo went across the cells and then came closer and closer to the cell of the four men, Fosi had to think of something fast as this was his only chance at escaping. Dacawo was now one cell away and Fosi looked to Adam who looked extremely tired after nights of sleeplessness, that's when he realised what he would tell Dacawo and as the lead guard came ever so closer, he finally reached the cell of the four men. "Okay men I have come to drop off your food, one small meal for each of you and that is all," said Dacawo.

CHAPTER 20

THE FINAL DAY

As Dacawo opened the cell door, he handed the men the food that they ever so needed, one by one the men grabbed the meal which was wrapped in a cloth. "Wait, Dacawo I need something for one of my cellmates, Adam hasn't been able to sleep for weeks now and will require some sleeping pills. So please I beg of you it is affecting the rest of us so can you at least provide him with two sleeping pills. One for today and one for tomorrow" begged Fosi. Dacawo quickly grabbed Fosi by the neck and pinned him to the floor, Fosi then struggled to breathe, "sleeping pills? Sleeping pills? You're lucky to be alive you nacas, Hooyo Macaan feeds you and clothes you and you want to behave like this you useless man. Don't ever ask me for sleeping pills or I'll kill you on the spot," screamed Dacawo. "Wait," said Abdirahman "we're all going to be affected by this Dacawo, Fosi's not lying to you, he stays up at night speaking to himself and he cannot sleep which is why he needs the pills so please find it in your heart to do this. And if this spreads to us then you won't be able to have prisoners to work in the yard when the new season comes in, we would be weak and tired". Dacawo slowly let go of Fosi's neck. "Tired and weak? I don't want any of you being tired and weak,

I want you all to be strong and to be ready for work in the coming months. Which is why I was going to give you the pills when you first asked Fosi," said Dacawo "Here's four pills you idiot, now keep them for your friend before he sleeps and I don't want anyone in the cell hearing about this little incident or Hooyo Macaan will have me killed! Hooyo Macaan and the rest of us will be in the other caves tonight for a feast however you won't be alone in the cells. My dogs will be looking after the cells just in case you try any funny business of stealing food or worse, planning to escape".

The men knew that Dacawo made up the lie of the feast they were having, this was to hide the fact that the cannibals were staying in the caves because of the eclipse. Dacawo then slowly left the premises and the entire prison, he kept laughing as he exited the prison doors and left the men who were to plan an escape that very night.

Fosi breathed in and out harshly after his life was nearly taken by the small but fierce guard who had almost killed him, he looked at the ceiling of the cell which was covered by spikes and stinging nettles.

The moon could be sited and the rest of the men looked on at Fosi, still on the ground after an hour he lay there smiling because the leader and the person they put their trust in for this escape knew, that what he prayed for was granted. Fosi quickly put the sleeping pills in his pocket and gave two to Adam for safekeeping, this was the key for their escape and he quickly gathered the men in a huddle. "Listen, men, we finally completed the task of getting the pills that we needed to escape this hell hole, and now Warsame will enter the prison as planned to give us the details of where we will all meet up".

CHAPTER 21

THE CALL

Abdirahman looked down while grinding his teeth and then spoke "What about my son? How are we going to take him out of this prison?". Fosi put both of his hands on Abdirahman's shoulders while shaking in fear, "listen, brother, don't you worry Warsame will be here very soon to tell me and you about the whereabouts of our loved ones. So, fear not and put your trust in Allah Abdirahman we will all get through this very soon". The other men watched on, this made them even more nervous especially Adam who was on the other side of the cell, thinking into space about what would happen to them if they got caught. Fosi went over to the young man and comforted him, "Listen here Adam you are one of the strongest people I know, so please do not despair, you will escape and prove everyone wrong so brother have faith that we will escape without any harm". As the conversation was going on between Fosi and Adam the prison doors were ordered to be opened for none other than a delivery from Warsame, he masked the visit as an excuse to deliver a letter to his brother before his execution, as he walked towards the cell of the men he could see his brother was successfully inside before the final escape, Warsame was wearing a white cloth around his head and face with a white macawiis (men's dress) , he slowly removed the head covering when he got to the cell. His emotions nearly got the better of him however he remained calm, he gave the letter to his brother and as the other guards watched his every move Warsame didn't risk putting the escape in danger and quickly left the premises. Cawaale opened the letter and realised it wasn't for him, it was for Fosi and the letter had the instructions of what the group had to do on the night of the escape. He quickly closed the letter and handed it to Fosi, the men then watched on as Fosi opened the letter and read it. The letter read "The eclipse will be at approximately 1:09 am and the cannibals including Hooyo Macaan will retreat to the top of the cave at 12:30 am on the 25th of July, Abdirahman's wife has been ordered to another city which I do not know of, so she will not be present to look after their child. Ali who is the child of Abdirahman has been taken to a nearby cave and I will be retrieving him and Fosi's father. He along with Abdirahman's child will be waiting at our escape route with a truck ready to leave for Hargeisa. By now you have hopefully taken my brother Cawaale out of his cell and into yours, and now your job will be to escape the prison and head towards the escape route which will be approximately a 2-minute walk from the prison. You will be able to identify the escape route by going east after leaving the prison doors, keep walking east and you will see woods with a path. Do not go around them but through them and you will see our truck parked on the cliffs. Make sure you light something as everywhere will be dark due to the eclipse and stay safe guys, I will see you on the outside,". They had finally received the call for the escape and when Fosi had finished reading he wept as he could not control himself, his father would be on the outside waiting to see him after so many years. He owed this all to the brave men in the cell as well as Warsame. Cawaale came to comfort Fosi as well, the other men joined in shedding tears of joy. Each one of those men had given there everything since they've been kept a prisoner in the prison. "Get up everyone, don't let the guards see you cry they may think we're up to something and this could sabotage our weeks of preparation," whispered Nasir as he held onto the bars of the cell. The guards started to panic in the yard and as they looked to the sky, they realised it was getting dark, Dacawo told the guards to calm down and let them know it wasn't time yet. As time went past, there was now approximately 1 hour before the retreat of the cannibals to Hooyo Macaan's cave. Dacawo had arrived back from his meeting with Hooyo Macaan in that time and came back with 2 dogs, they resembled the wild African dog.

They had brown fur, were skinny and had very large canines. Dacawo then walked up to the cell of the 4 men, "Listen here, I and the guards are going to have a meeting with Hooyo Macaan all night long, so I've left my best friends here to look after you. Remember this they are hungry so if any of you try stealing food or smuggling someone into your cell, you have bought this amongst yourselves".

The time was now 12:00 am and the guards along with Dacawo power walked to the doors of the prison and left, the irony was the four men knew what they meant by a 'meeting with Hooyo Macaan' and they now knew the time of escape was very close. The men were now all near the cell bars watching the sky as the eclipse was only 30 minutes away now and the time had come to escape.

CHAPTER 22

BREAKOUT

The time was now 00:45, and the time had come, "Everyone stand back, this is where the sleeping pills come into good use" said Fosi. He went straight into his pocket and clutched both sleeping pills, and then put one in each hand. He called the two dogs over to the cell they were trying to escape from, and they both ran with extreme speed. The dogs didn't bark but growled all while the fear in Adam made him squeal and scream "shhh don't make any noise my brothers" said Fosi. "Why are you calling the dogs over to us Fosi are you crazy?" Abdirahman said in an aggressive but quiet tone. "Just sit back and watch walalo" and that's when Fosi threw the first pill at the dog. The hunger of the first dog overwhelmed him and he quickly ate the pill, the second pill was then thrown, and the second dog leapt for the pill and swallowed it. The group all looked at each other in amazement; it took the dogs almost 5 minutes before they fell asleep. "They should be gone to sleep for the next 4 hours so let's be quick," said Fosi. Abdirahman looked at Fosi and was mesmerised at this, no wonder he wanted the pills so badly thought Abdirahman so that he could pull off one of the most amazing things he has ever witnessed. The dogs then went to sleep, their paws stretched out as they lay in the almost dark prison. The region was getting darker, and the eclipse was slowly covering the moon, Fosi went into his pocket and took at out a brown key, he had assembled many cadays' to carve it into the shape of Dacawo's key for the duration he was in the cell. The men couldn't believe what they were witnessing, everything Fosi had been doing for the duration they were in their cells had a meaning and a massive purpose.

"Bismillah (in the name of Allah)" Fosi said before entering the makeshift key into the lock, he slowly turned it and opened the cell door, one by one avoiding the paws of the dogs as they snored, the men then slowly exited the cell. Nasir was second after Fosi to exit and he took a deep breath in, even though they were receiving the same air within the cell as the outside, Nasir felt like he had breathed in the new fresh air.

Adam and Cawaale came after, Adam cried without making any noise, tears dripped down his face as he now knew that he was free, he couldn't wait to return to Aden and be seen as a hero.

Abdirahman was last, flashbacks of the day he had escaped the cell and Ali telling him to leave while he was left to die encapsulated his brain, he kept blaming himself for that day but tonight it was different, he would leave with his father and carry on Ali's legacy through his son he had named after him. The men all stood in the middle of the prison walls known to them as the yard. The other prisoners could be heard snoring on the opposite wing; they had almost forgotten that this wasn't even the start of the escape. However, this felt amazing to the men all those months and years for some of them went past in those cells, and the guards who would bully them and treat them as slaves were over for just those minutes.

Fosi then picked up two rocks from the floor and ignited them by rubbing both rocks between each other, he then lit his Cadey from the top and a huge light lit up as the eclipse finally engulfed the moon and darkness spread throughout the prison. It was finally here a total eclipse of the region had finally come, Adam began to cry and panic as the only thing that was lighting his life was the Cadey.

"Calm down Adam, now listen to me guys everyone grab someone's shoulder I will lead from the front and guide us out of the prison door, I have another key for the door in my left pocket so whoever is behind me which looks like it is Nasir hold my torch so I can unlock the door".

So then the men moved, all together now each one grabbing the others shoulder with both hands, praying that they make it out alive into the free world. They had now finally reached the prison door, Fosi gave the torch over to Nasir and then took the second key out of his left pocket. Surprisingly this key was Dacawo's spare key for the prison door. Fosi had swiped it from him while Dacawo was hitting him within the cell after he had asked for the pills. He slowly put the key into the prison door and unlocked it, they then made their way out and Fosi then took the torch from Nasir's hand again. Now they truly smelt freedom, they now had to look for the escape route that Warsame had told Fosi in the letter, they would have to walk east from the prison.

CHAPTER 23

THE ECLIPSE

Tripping, tumbling and getting back up was the pattern of the men's journey to freedom, cuts and bruises filled their feet, they had no light guiding them from the bottom but only the top using Fosi's torch. They walked for almost an hour now and there was no sign of any wood path which leads them to an escape route; They started to feel hopeless and tired. Until Fosi saw a light beaming from in between a few trees and as they got closer, he realised it was the woods they were looking for, the entrance of the woods were scary, insects surrounded the woods, and the sound of wild animals could be heard from the branches of the trees. They continued to walk as insects touched their bare feet and felt the wind of the night brush past their legs. Adam squealed and shivered as he walked, Cawaale's fears also got the better of him and held his eyes so he couldn't see the surrounding terror. The three remaining men didn't feel any sort of fear, maybe because of the torment they had already been through in the past, Fosi then realised that he could see the headlights of the truck in the distance and the men moved ever so closer to freedom, cries of a baby could then be heard and a hooded figure holding the baby could be seen too.

Abdirahman cried and couldn't hold his emotions in, he ran to his baby and even though he knew Warsame was holding him, he didn't care.

He ran and ran tumbling again but getting up after every fall; He was now ahead of the group as the rest of them walked at their normal pace. He finally got out of the woods and arrived in front of the truck near the cliffs, the cliffs were high up and the view of the towns could be seen, Warsame stood there next to the car door with Ali in his arms. "Warsame we have finally made it lets get going brother," said Abdirahman.

Something was very odd though, Warsame wouldn't speak and continued to look at the floor all while the hood hid his face. He then slowly took off his hood and something happened which made Abdirahman shake in fear.

It wasn't Warsame holding the baby, it was Hooyo Macaan, and she screamed with laughter, "Warya, you thought you could escape me? You will never escape me" she screamed. "Where is Warsame said Abdirahman, where is he? He lied to me! He's betrayed us again!" he screamed. It was too late for the other men, they had also arrived and realised it was Hooyo Macaan, Adam fainted in fear and Cawaale went on his knees and cried in terror. "He didn't betray you, he's in the back seat of the truck and I will punish him after I punish every single one of you standing in front of me right now".

Hooyo Macaan was wearing a black dirac and cut her hair short, she stared at Fosi who was in the back behind Abdirahman and smiled. "You're probably wondering who told us about your escape and it was someone in your circle, someone you thought you could trust!". Abdirahman was left confused as to who would tell Hooyo Macaan about the escape, who could it be he thought.

He looked behind him and everyone remained quiet. "No, I don't believe you, I will never believe you, you're a liar, these are my friends and family they will never betray me". Hooyo Macaan grinned and looked to the floor. "Edo come here stand next to me and tell your son the truth about who you are". Nasir slowly stepped forward and for the first time, he held his head high. He stood right next to Hooyo Macaan, and he didn't look at her face once. Abdi kneeled on the floor in shock and so did the other men.

CHAPTER 24

THE LIAR

"Listen, Abdirahman it's not what it looks like trust me. I did this to save you so please do not take it harshly". Abdirahman bit his tongue so hard that blood started to flow from his mouth and then spoke "You're supposed to be my father, and you betrayed me the only person I have left is you and you do this? How could you do this?". "Your father has always been by my side Abdirahman, I found him as a child lost in the desert and took him in as my own and fed him, clothed him of the food you all eat as I didn't want him to be like us because I had a different plan for him. When he reached 18, I sent him into Hargeisa to learn your people's trade, he took on a new name and fake parents were with him every step of the way acting as if he's their own to fool everyone. Until he went to the UK, at first when he told me I was excited for him due to the fact I wanted to start my trade across the globe after I took over British Somaliland. But when he came back with that stupid British officer, he spoiled my plans of domination. They thought they could steal from me, but I was waiting right behind them every step of the way. However, you need to understand he then made me very angry because he ran away with his friend Officer Stevens and betrayed me, he thought he could escape me after he found out the type of person I am. He then fled to Las Canood and started hunting down my workers across the country. He then escaped again and fled back to Hargeisa disguised as an officer with officer Stevens. Again, creating a life for himself with your mother. He said he was on his way with Officer Stevens to the UK, well that's what he told your mother but that was all a lie, he wanted to defeat me and had planned to kill me. Imagine the woman that gave him everything he wanted to kill, that's why I killed his best friend officer Stevens right in front of his eyes and imprisoned him to this day. Now that's the true story Abdirahman". Hooyo Macaan looked at Nasir with disgust and sat down on the floor with Ali. "Why did you do this Aabo?" cried Abdirahman. "I knew Hooyo Macaan would find us she's smart Abdirahman, she's always one step ahead of us I had to tell her we were planning an escape, so I let Dacawo know from the night before. I care about you and your son Abdirahman but don't worry we can all be alive back in our cell, because we will never make it out of here alive" said Nasir. "Now that's not the whole truth Abdirahman, you really think I would fear your father? He could come with an army and I would still defeat him,

I was never bothered about him taking a letter with my hunter's names on it. There was more in that box that your father isn't telling you,". Hooyo Macaan looked into Nasir's eyes and finally let out the truth about the box. "Listen Abdirahman, there's more in that box than just a letter. When officer Stevens and I finally retrieved the box, we tried to destroy it by hitting it against the floor. But something unbelievable happened, the bottom base of the box smashed open and a bracelet fell out. It was the most beautiful bracelet we had ever laid our eyes on. It had gemstones on it that we'd only heard about in stories. Rubies, diamonds and emeralds filled the bracelet, and we knew that this was designed by an expert. We quickly fixed the box and sealed it inside the compartment, we then agreed to split the money once we had sold it on the black market, but we had to defeat Hooyo Macaan's listeners beforehand. Years went by and after defeating her listeners, I started a family in Hargeisa and the birth of you made me so happy. We knew if we were to be completely free from Hooyo Macaan, we would have to defeat her so that's why I left the box with you Abdirahman because I knew if anything had happened to me you would be able to find and start a life with that bracelet. Somehow Hooyo Macaan's listeners managed to track you down, and that's when she sent Sharmarke to lure you to her caves. She failed the first time, but she didn't give up". "Dacawo hand me the box now, let me show these people how much the treasure they stole meant to me," said Hooyo Macaan. Dacawo then slowly handed Hooyo Macaan the box that held her most prized possession. She then proceeded to smash the box onto the floor; everyone could now see the bracelet on the floor in its beauty. The gems on the bracelet glistened in the night of the eclipse, shining brighter than the truck's headlights. She picked it up and attached it to her left wrist, and for the first time, she shed a tear. "This was given to me by my husband on the night of an eclipse, he designed it in the caves for over 3 months before our wedding. The day that he had given it to me was the best day of my life, the way he had put it on my wrist when our marriage was finalised, our years together and the children we had was something I will never forget. He died fighting intruders who wanted to banish us from these caves, they should have just left us alone, but they didn't you see, and you and your British friend stole the only thing I had to remember him by,". For the first time in their lives, the group witnessed Hooyo Macaan cry, they didn't know what to do but look on and watch at her tears hit the desert floor. Abdirahman had no emotion on his face as he looked into his father's eyes, his father had jeopardised his family's life for a bracelet. He could see the shame and guilt on his father's face as he kept looking away from his sons' stare, Nasir knew the truth would come out one day and the gamble he took now showed it didn't pay off.

"Dacawo open the door for that useless boy Warsame he has some explaining to do". Warsame was then let out of the truck by Dacawo, his mouth and hands were tied, and he had tears rolling down his face, this was a surprising sight. Abdirahman had never seen Warsame like this but what made it more confusing was that Warsame was not the one that ruined the plan it was his own father. Dacawo then removed the cloth he wrapped around Warsame's mouth and he was then presented in front of the men, he was standing side by side with Nasir who had now been known as the traitor.

"Now what I want you to do Warsame is explain to Fosi why his father's not here with us today, go on tell him quickly," said Hooyo Macaan. Warsame wiped the tears off his face while still tied "Listen Fosi she made me do it, she made me do it I tell you she made me do it" argued Warsame. "Enough Warsame tell your friend where his father is and why you wasted his time here for all those years" shouted Hooyo Macaan. Warsame then took a deep breath "Your father's right in front of you Fosi, your father is Nasir".

CHAPTER 25

THE TRUTH

Everyone went silent due to the shock of what they had just heard. Warsame then spoke "When Nasir was fleeing from Hooyo Macaan he made a stop in Las Canood and a wonderful family took care of him, your grandfather brought him in and kept him safe and when he died his daughter had no one and he vowed to protect her which led him to marry her and they then had you,". Nasir then punched Warsame to the ground. "You lied to me, you come to tell me that Fosi's my son? How could this be? And Edo (auntie) you knew all of this; how could you do this?" Nasir screamed. "Enough warya! yes I made Warsame bring your child Fosi to me because I wanted to kill him before he could find and kill me, and obviously to get back at what you did to me with your little officer friend, now after that family reunion it's time to reunite all of you in the afterlife,". The men could see the view of the rest of the desert and the small town from the high cliff that they were on, Dacawo then took out his pistol from his pocket and pointed it at Warsame's head after getting him off the ground. Adam and Cawaale had never seen anything like this before; they were left speechless as they sat on the floor and glared at the distance amongst the cliff; They were higher than they had ever been, and the beauty of the view had been disrupted by the horrors of Hooyo Macaan. "Now this is what's going to happen Abdirahman, you have now found a new sibling in this world and also a not so great father, so I'm going to give you a question, answer it incorrectly and I will kill either your father or your brother.

However, if you answer them right, I will imprison them again. So, you now have the choice to save your family members. Before we do that, Dacawo do the honours and get this man out of my sight". A loud bang erupted from the pistol, and there he was lying face-first on the floor with blood leaking from his head, it was Warsame who had been killed in cold blood all while his hands were still wrapped in the evil people's cloth.

Abdirahman cried and the rest of the men looked away at his body, he wasn't even given a chance to hug his brother. Cawaale couldn't hold back his tears and ran at Dacawo in quick succession but it was too late, Hooyo Macaan had grabbed his leg, picked him up and walked over to the edge of the cliff.

"This is what happens when you betray me," she said as she threw him off the steep cliffs of the Somali desert and walked slowly back to where she was sat. She picked up the baby that she placed on the floor before she committed the horrific attack and had no emotion on her face. "Now where were we warya, oh yes, the questions. If you answer them correctly, I will not kill you and your family, I'll even spare your Arab friend who is shaking behind you, now the first question is what is my real name?".

Abdirahman was left confused, how could he answer such a question about what her real name was, everyone, called her Hooyo Macaan because she nurtured and cared for all her hunters like a mother. Dacawo looked at her and was confused himself, this was impossible and Abdirahman was left hopeless with this question as he sweated in the night's heat. "Your name is, your name I…" Abdirahman kept stuttering as he repeated that line. "My name is what?" she laughed. He knew he had failed as tears dropped from his eyes, his father looked him in the eyes and whispered, "don't worry".

Dacawo was then ordered to point the gun at Fosi's head, Dacawo then closed his eyes and pulled the trigger. But something was different; there was no bang and Dacawo realised he had run out of bullets. He kept pulling the trigger, but no bullets were entering Fosi's skull, "today's not your day, Adam come here and get me some water from the truck, me and Dacawo are thirsty". Adam slowly made his way to the truck, his knees were shaking as he made his way to serve Hooyo Macaan, he then tripped due to the fear in his heart. "Look at you you're useless now go and get my water," said Hooyo Macaan as she gripped his shirt while he lay on the floor. He finally got back up from after she had released her claws from his shirt.

He then got to the truck and retrieved the water bottles from the boot, while he handed them their drinks he went back to his position in dismay. They drank and drank in the heat while they got ready to execute Fosi. Dacawo tied Fosi's eyes and hands and made him walk to the edge of the cliff and Hooyo Macaan followed. When they arrived on the edge of the cliff Hooyo Macaan asked Fosi if he had any final words, but he didn't respond at all.

All Fosi did was recite the shahada (pledge of faith) from his tongue. Abdirahman and Nasir couldn't look on as they witnessed their newly found family member being executed in front of their eyes, he was seconds away from being thrown from the cliff which was so high up.

Hooyo Macaan stretched and then wiped her mouth due to the sweat which dripped down her face, all the men then looked away. Abdirahman was kneeling in the other direction with his baby in his arms, Nasir sat behind the truck and looked in the opposite direction.

But Adam continued to look on at the execution. Minutes passed and Abdirahman heard no screams from Fosi and no shouting from Dacawo or Hooyo Macaan, the execution seemed to be a quiet one and Abdirahman's heart ached for his newly found brother's execution.

CHAPTER 26

CLIFFHANGER

Twenty minutes had passed and Abdirahman was in the same position looking in the other direction until he felt a hand touch his shoulder. He looked back and couldn't believe what he was seeing, it was Adam carrying Fosi. In the distance, he could see Dacawo and Hooyo Macaan passed out on the floor with the wind blowing her dress. Abdirahman quickly got up and squeezed Fosi like never before, "How could this be? How?" shouted Abdirahman. Adam then took the blindfold off of Fosi, he had been severely beaten by Hooyo Macaan just before they tried to execute him "I could ask you the same question, how did this happen? why am I still alive?" said Fosi as he looked at Adam. "I put the pills into the water bottles Fosi, I still had them from the prison cells, and I knew it would help us later. This was our only chance at survival and alhamdullilah we have survived". Fosi then looked into Adam's eyes and hugged him. "See I knew you were always smart Adam don't ever doubt yourself again walalo". The men made their way to the truck and saw that Nasir looked up at the men, he finally knew that they had defeated Hooyo Macaan, but he didn't say anything. The guilt of what he had done still sat with him, Abdirahman and Fosi didn't hug their father but looked at him and told him that they needed to get out of where they were and fast. They checked the truck but before Hooyo Macaan had collapsed, she took the brakes and acceleration apart so they couldn't escape, the men decided to pack enough water and walk the rest of the miles to the main road and hitchhike back to Hargeisa. Before they went, Fosi, Adam and Nasir went over to where the bodies of Hooyo Macaan and Dacawo lay and decided to put them in the truck and throw them off the cliff, to finally end the torment of the two monsters. They struggled to carry Hooyo Macaan due to her large weight, however, Dacawo was very easy to carry, but they finally loaded them onto the back of the truck and tied their feet and hands with pieces of cloth. Abdirahman was in the distance away from the cliff holding Ali, he kissed the cheeks of his son as the other men were at work. "Listen, men we have to push the truck off the cliff now so let's get ready and remember this torment is finally over once that truck goes off the cliff," said Nasir as he breathed in and out heavily. The men got ready and then started to push the truck, however, it wouldn't move. Nasir realised the handbrake was still up and went inside the truck to check, he tried releasing the handbrake, but it was stuck and wouldn't go down. The truck would only move inch by inch with all their force and Nasir decided to tell them to keep pushing while he tried to release the handbrake from within. "Listen, men, I will stay inside the truck with the door open to hold the handbrake down and then jump out before it gets to the cliff". "You can't do this Aabo" said Fosi, while the men looked at each other. Fosi had finally found out who is father was and didn't want to see him risk his life so quickly, but Nasir refused and told him he had to do it to make things right. So, Nasir went into the front seat of the truck and held the handbrake down, the car then began to roll. As the car rolled, he felt a hand touch his shoulder and begin to touch his neck. Hooyo Macaan had woken up and grabbed him, biting into his shoulder. He grabbed her and they fought within the car, Fosi and Adam had realised what was going on so they ran to the front door of the truck before it could fall off the cliff. As they tried to board the front seat Nasir kept shouting at them to stay away. Abdirahman saw what was happening and put baby Ali down and joined the other men to save his father. Hooyo Macaan tried to escape the truck but Nasir held her back to stop her from killing his sons, "Let me go" she screamed as the car continued to roll away the men watched on from the distance. Nasir uttered the shahada as the truck slowly fell from the cliff and the men cried while they watched on. Fosi witnessed his newly found father die saving their lives and the future of the Somalis who would have been a victim to Hooyo Macaan. They all hugged each other in a group, their tears dropped to the ground while they looked on as the truck hit the floor and burst into flames. They sat in the desert until midday thinking and contemplating about what they had just witnessed. Warsame, Cawaale and Nasir all died saving them. Abdirahman then looked to his left and saw the broken box which was on the floor of where Hooyo Macaan was sitting before she was killed; he knew the contents of this and placed it into his pocket. "We must leave now guys before the other hunters realise where their queen has gone, and to be safe we need to head to Burco with new identities for a while," said Fosi. Abdirahman smiled as he knew he was in good hands; his brother was with him, but the memories of his father continued to take over his mind. The men walked hours with baby Ali towards the main road, when they had finally reached the main road Adam said "brothers it has been a pleasure knowing you all, but I will now head to Berbera and take a boat back to Aden. I fully appreciate what you have both done for me, I can finally go back to my family and tell them of the tale that I have lived and the way that I survived a nightmare".

The two men hugged each other and both Abdirahman and Fosi now knew they had found a good friend in Adam, but now he was to leave for Yemen.

"What about the bracelet?" said Adam before he left. "It has been destroyed along with Hooyo Macaan now Adam, and it is best for everyone that it stays that way," said Fosi. Adam shed a tear as he waved for a truck on its way to Berbera, he climbed at the back and continued to look back as tears rolled down his face as the truck left for Berbera.

A few moments later a family car came across Abdirahman and Fosi and the man driving saw how badly injured Fosi was. He then asked him what had happened and Fosi told the family they were lost in the desert for some time and had been attacked by thieves.

The family quickly allowed the two men and the baby into the car destined for Burco, and as Abdirahman sat in the back seat, he took the broken box and the letter out from his pocket and smiled because he was finally free from the nightmare he thought would never end.

PRESENT DAY

The young boy was speechless; He had never heard a story so gripping and mesmerising. He was scared at first, but his grandfather told him to sit next to him and hugged him. "Don't worry it is just a story," the old man said. The young boy stared at his grandfather, who sat calmly on his bed while holding the book he had just read.

The boy's father had finally arrived back and entered the room, "Nasir go to sleep warya, it is getting late and it is almost midnight," said his father. "Aabo you look tired you need some rest as well, thank you for looking after him for me while we were gone for so long,". "No problem Ali, anything for my grandson," said the old man, Ali and his father then looked at each other and smiled while Nasir ran over to his father and hugged him.

The room was then left alone to Abdirahman who placed the book in his drawer right next to the box; He picked the box up went over to the front yard and buried it. He then went back to his bed and lay there all while looking up at the white ceilings above. "It's finally over," he said and went to sleep.

THE END

Printed in Great Britain
by Amazon